SHE-WOLF
She-Wolf – Book 1

Diana Philbrick

SHE-WOLF
She-Wolf – Book 1

FETISH WORLD BOOKS

Introduction

In her dream, a wolf was tearing chunks from her body, and she was screaming, pulling at the straps that bound her. The pain was horrible, but it was her helplessness that begat her rage, and it was her rage that kept her sane. She focused on the sweat dripping off her nipples and reminded herself that it was the hook-and-collar, the nipple weights, and the darkness of her dungeon cell that were the cause of her suffering.

…And the legit.

The legion's commander, the legate, had ordered Sextus to "pacify" her for her deflowering, and this torture, this horrific agony was the direct result of that command. *Legatus Legionis* Lucius Flaccus had the right to fuck any slave girl he wanted, including virgins.

The right to fuck…

Who were these monsters who thought they had could kill and enslave innocent people? How did they justify their crimes, their perversions? Writing a law did not make it right, it only made it Roman, and she hated all things Roman. She had never even heard of Rome before the legionaries invaded her village and killed her father. She had never known anyone who would kill a woman in retaliation. The Romans had crucified her mother as payback for the legionaries he had killed defending his home. It had taken her a full day to die on their Roman cross. When she did mercifully pass, Sextus turned to her and pronounced her punishment.

"Put the pup in with my dogs," he had ordered. "If they don't eat her, she can live with the beasts until she's ripe enough for the block."

The vicious mastiffs, which the Romans used to guard their camp, could have easily ripped out her throat, but instead, for some unknown reasons, they had welcomed her into their space, shared their food and water, and kept her warm with their bodies. The dogs saved her.

Not that she knew it at the time. For weeks, she did not care what the Romans did to her; she had been numb, dazed with grief over the murder of her parents. Perhaps the dogs sensed her lack of fear and responded to it. They treated her like one of them, and she began to think of them as her family. At Sextus's order, she ate, slept, suffered, and ran naked with the beasts—all to the great amusement of the Romans—which resulted in her acquiring unusual strength and speed, hunter instincts, and a killer's temperament. The dogs also taught her caution and patience—from them she learned that to exact revenge she needed to survive, and to do that she needed to act like a cowed pet, a beaten cur until...

A sharp pain in her shoulder made her cry out in the darkness.

"Make sure she is suitably cowed when you send her to me," she remembered Flaccus ordering his chief torturer, the legion's *dux carnifex*, and Sextus nodding dutifully.

Suitably cowed...!

This was the way high-born Roman commander spoke. It kept them at an arms-length from the dirty business of torture and execution. She understood his fear—in many ways, she was an animal, too wild and too "gamey" for a patrician like him to tame.

Sextus had immediately ordered his men to restrain her with the fearsome hook-and-collar, which turned the

6

natural curve in her back into an exaggerated arch. They then carried her to the dungeon where they raised her bound arms behind in a cruel strappado. The combination of the ass hook and the strappado was unbearable, forcing her to choose between agonizing shoulder pain and impalement. The only relief came when she stood on her toes, but this was only temporary.

If only they knew what was in her head, she thought, the torture would be worse.

In defiance of their rules, she had learned Latin by listening closely to the men talking as she lay on the floor with the dogs. The law forbid slaves learning the Roman language beyond a few basic commands.

A sudden burst of pain in her tits forced her to her toes. She recognized Sextus's handiwork in the pain. Ironically, he had earned his well-deserved reputation by allowing his torture victims an opportunity to retreat occasionally from their pain. This built their hope that they could survive his torture. A victim needed hope, she thought, as another wave of agony surged through her body.

"Be friendly, sympathize with them, give them the idea that they will survive...," he told the aspirants he trained as legion torturers. "A successful interrogation is all about refocusing the prisoner's thoughts. Even when the objective is punishment and not interrogation, controlling thoughts and being attentive to the details will produce better results."

Details...

Her torture was a good example of his attention to detail. He had made tiny loops from rawhide strips and used them to hang heavy weights from her nipples. It was a detail that created the backdrop of suffering over which he laid the sharp stabbing pain.

"Details…," Sextus had repeated to the attentive students watching. "These weights will keep our Taexali dog-girl in pain no matter how she turns her body."

All this agony simply to please the legate…

Slaves had no rights in the Rumabo slave depot, but it was traditional that no one, not even the officers fucked a virgin. It was a practical constraint not a moral one—virgins were simply worth too much on the block with their hymens intact to waste on a man's momentary pleasure. Most of the time, they honored this tradition, but occasionally, when a slave girl aroused the legate, he indulged.

She had seen the look in his eyes as he passed by her dog cage. Each day, he had lingered longer, staring at her naked body. Once, when Sextus had her out on the chain with the dogs preparing for a hunt, Flaccus had stopped and stared at her for a long time, his eyes traveling along her naked body, taking in her long lean muscles, her hard ass and tits, her long neck. He gaze had lingered on her face, savoring the harsh Celtic angles and plains.

She had tried to hide her loathing from him, her hatred of all things Roman, but her indifference came across as arousal. In truth, she was curious—no man had penetrated her yet and she did wonder what it would be like. Sextus had been careful to preserve her virginity for the block, but he could not protect it or her from Rumabo's randy commander.

Protect her…

She was still thinking about her strange choice of words, Roman words, when Sextus reentered the cell carrying a torch. He ran his hands over her bare shoulders

8

and felt her straining muscles trembling; he checked the tension of the hook-and-collar by lifting the chain; then he tested the effectiveness of the weights by pulling down on the cords.

"He will sell you immediately after the deflowering, my pet," he whispered, running his hands along her flanks. "*Legatus* Lucius Flaccus does not keep the slaves he fucks around for long. The rumor is that he doesn't want anyone to know anything about his sexual performance."

He did not know she could understand Latin. He was like a man talking to his horse.

"I don't think that of course—the commander is a powerful man, a prime example of Roman virility. There is always ugly and loose talk in the ranks about a legion's commander's fucking."

Sextus had had too much to drink and was talking too freely, even if he assumed he was speaking to a dumb animal.

"The legate enjoys inflicting pain, especially on innocent creatures like you, Xara. People think I am a monster for the work I do, for the care I take in performing my duties, but I am simply doing a job. I am…like the men who clean the latrines or those who cook our food. Does anyone accuse them of begin demons because they do their work…well…with…pride? Do they?"

He was beginning to slur his words. She knew he would pass out soon, leaving her to suffer, but the germ of an idea was forming in her mind.

"I would have…kept you…as my pet…forever," he mumbled. "You were a fitting companion…for…my dogs, but I cannot go…against the…"

9

Chapter One – First Kill

The can struck her bare leg and sent a sliver of pain into her brain. She wanted to scream, but her pride made her accept the agony without reacting. Sextus has used a log whip on her and the dogs. Compared to the feel of his braided leather on a bare back, the legate's cane was nothing.

He struck her again on the flanks, three times.

Flaccus was not the kind of man who admired pride in a slave. He wanted her terrorized, pacified, and submissive. He could have simply ordered her to walk faster—and like any good slave girl, she would have complied instantly—but in his mind pain was an essential part of deflowering a girl. A slave who accepted pain without expressing it was being resistant—something he could not allow. Fear, he often said, was the basis of Roman conquest and rule. Without it, the empire's millions of slaves would revolt, and there would be chaos, disorder, and savagery in the land…as there was before the Romans came, ergo, fear was good.

Xara suddenly realized the stupidity of her stoicism and glanced back at him with terror on her face. He smiled at her surrender and struck her again to emphasize that he always punished resistance even after surrender.

He had brought terror into her eyes, he thought, but she was still refusing to scream.

Instilling fear in a slave destined for sexual service was essential. How else could her new owner control a strong and supple beauty like this? He had ordered Sextus to pacify her, but he could see that the torture had not had the desired effect. He would have to do it himself. As the commander of the legion stationed at Rumabo Imperium, everything, from the maintenance of the stockade wall to the disciplining of a resistant slave girl, was ultimately his responsibility.

He laid a series of vicious strokes on her legs, eliciting a brief yelp, but it was still too little for his liking. He needed to be careful though, he reasoned, too much caning and he would need to delay her sale, which would mean gossip; a commander could not afford to have his men think he was weak, even in the use of his cock. Not only that, but he was the commander of a slave depot and needed to constantly exhibit his expertise with the creatures. Any bloody fool could beat a girl like Xara into submission, but the goal was to instill fear without crushing her spirit. It was this mixture of fear and spirit that made fucking such a beautiful sub-human like her so special. It was this combination that got them the best auction price.

Inflicting such targeted pain took the experience of a seasoned professional like him. He should never have left this girl's preparations to Sextus; the man was a genius with interrogation and punishment, but in matters requiring more subtlety, he was a disaster.

Her flashing legs distracted him for a moment. Sextus had delivered her a *subligaria*, a white loincloth, with the hook-and-collar still attached and her arms bound tightly behind her back at the wrists and elbows. The loincloth was a nice touch, he decided. It would be red with her blood when he finished…clear evidence of the power of his cock, power befitting the commander of the Ninth Legion.

The commander of the Ninth Legion…!

11

Emperor Hadrian had once personally awarded him the *corona aurea* for outstanding service in the conquest of southern Briton. He was a hero of Rome, one of her favorite sons. His command of the Rumabo Imperium, the largest fort and slave depot in Briton had been a fitting reward for his years of loyal service. A fitting reward…which came with many benefits and privileges such as the one he was now enjoying.

He struck her again on the thigh and her body jerked back with a cry of sudden pain. Better, he thought! A deflowering without a suitable amount of pain was…un-roman. It was traditional that he terrorize her right up to the moment of his penetration.

Tradition…

Tradition was important to we Romans. It connected the past with the future. It formed the bedrock on which our superior Roman civilization rested, the glue that held the empire together. Tradition and fear…two sides of the Roman coin.

He struck another fierce blow to the backs of her bare thighs, and she responded with a full-throated scream. Now they were getting somewhere, he thought; however, there was still something wrong with her reaction.

Was it anger…? Was it possible he had heard anger in her scream?

The thought was irrational and disconcerting, yet it lingered. After a night of torture at Sextus's hands, she should be as pliant as a whipped dog. Could she be trying to resist in the only way a slave could resist—by holding her feelings inside? If so, it was totally unacceptable, and he would need to deal with it immediately. He could not allow a Rumabo slave girl, especially one destined for sexual service to express any feeling other than a sincere and almost pathological desire to serve her masters...certainly not anger.

He caned her again in anger and she scampered faster up the guardhouse steps, but still not fast enough for his liking. Admittedly, her hook-and-collar made quick movement painful, but the thought that she was resisting in some subtle way had taken root in his mind.

He clearly had his work cut out for him today.

He paused to enjoy the sight of her frantic movements, her desperate attempts to avoid the worst of his cane. Despite his resolve, the quickness of her legs, of her bare feet on the smooth stone, of her twisting torso were intoxicating. She was truly a beauty now that she was clean of the muck and scent of the Sextus's dogs. She was a black-haired minx, the daughter of a Briton bitch who Sextus had crucified in well-justified retribution for her husband's resistance. Xara would sell for a substantial sum at the auction, he imagined. He would have her stripped and suspended by her wrists outside the auction house where she would not only attract buyer interest in herself, but also promote the auction as a whole.

It was a brilliant promotional idea; perhaps it would be even better if she were in pain of some kind or perhaps wearing a chastity belt to suggest that her cunt was valuable...? He would ask the chief auctioneer his opinion. Using a well-formed girl like this to excite the interests of the international cadre of slave buyers who visited the fort was a well-worn but still effective tactic.

But that day was a way off. Today, he wanted her penetration to be perfect, not just for him, but also for her new master. Roman domination was her life now, and he wanted to be sure that there was integrity in her sale.

Grooming young slaves for the block took patience and commitment.

He moved quickly and struck her three more blows with the cane. The thought of those long, well-muscled limbs wrapped around his waist in coitus made him tremble with excitement. He had penetrated scores of virgins in the stone guardhouse, and he knew it was important that he keep tight control of his libido. The sexual excitement of fucking a slave girl virgin could be too much and result in premature ejaculation. It was easy to do—the stripping, the bondage, the requisite caning of soft thighs, and the spanking of a hard quivering ass could be too much for a man of his potency. Too much anticipation would work against him perhaps even cause him to embarrass himself, which would be a catastrophe. The men needed to respect their commander and that would be in danger of he came on himself.

Which was why he often brought beautiful slave girls to the stone building to fuck. It was far enough from the walls to hide any sexual missteps, but not too far to put himself in danger from the savages who continued to lurk outside the fort. Be patient, he reminded himself! Savor each bite of this juicy fruit slowly.

Good advice... It was hard, though, hard to resist such a ripe young body, hard for him to watch her bound body move in the hook-and-collar. Her bare shoulders and severely curved back preyed on his mind, making his cock as hard as stone. He wanted to lay his cane on her entire naked body and watch her writhe, listen to her cry and plead for his mercy, but the necessity of clear skin for the action block held him back.

Why should such practical matters constrain his pleasure, he asked himself? The legate should not be subject to such plebian concerns. They needed to find a way to keep his girls, the ones he fucked silent until their auction—perhaps a heavy leather hood with a good lock…? He would speak to the chief auctioneer about this idea as well. Xara's slim figure and her pointed tits and ass were inspiring him.

"Patience…," he whispered to himself. "She will be yours soon enough, begging for you."

She was a beauty all right, a trophy that would set any man's passions aflame; and he was plucking her at exactly the right moment, at the very peak of her sweet taste. He had been watching her for days in her cage and on her dog leash. Her time with Sextus's mastiffs had allowed her to ripen to just the right degree of hardness. He usually liked them softer, more nubile, but a firm fruit was often good as well. Perhaps other slave girls could profit by being with the dogs.

"She is too much of an animal for you, commander," Sextus had told him when he ordered her pacified. "She is practically one of the dogs now."

"Then it is up to you, *dux carnifex*, to prepare her for me," he had replied, annoyed.

Which he had not done, he thought. He could still sense her resistance. He flicked his wrist again and the cane flew twice into her ass cheeks. The unique whopping sound of wood on bare flesh was satisfying. There was nothing else like it. She reached the guardhouse door and stopped then turned to face him with her head down, too scared to look into his eyes. It was a good start.

He caned her hard under her breasts through the tunic. He wanted to hear her scream again. She twisted and cringed deliciously under the barrage, but her screams were still inadequate. Incredibly, she was still defiantly

15

trying to hide her pain from him. He shoved her to the side, unlocked the door, and pushed her roughly inside. He didn't want the guards on the wall watching him punish her. Command privilege, especially when it involved a young female savage, fostered jealousy among the men, which for a stationary legion like the Ninth was potential trouble.

He pushed her to the middle of the room then sat in one of the room's chairs. Her eyes, wide with fear and pain, darted in every direction. This was better, much better. He always enjoyed the quiet moments when their imaginations stoked their panic. The terror of young girls excited him. He reached out with the long cane and lifted the side of her tunic. She had an extraordinarily high and hard ass, he thought, just the way he liked them. She trembled with the cane so close but remained still as he brought it down hard on her shapely leg. She is an incredibly exciting beauty, he thought again.

"STRIP," he ordered.

Struggling, with her arms bound behind her back, she loosened the cloth at her waist and let it fall to the floor exposing her nakedness then stood still as he inspected her body. Every part of her fit beautifully on her lean frame, all with eye-pleasing proportionality. The painful bending of her back—forced by the hook-and-collar—enhanced her long sensual line.

"Spread your legs and turn...SLOWLY. I want to enjoy you before we start."

She didn't move. He might have been testing her, but more likely, he had forgotten that slaves did not speak Latin. Flaccus smiled then struck her inner thighs and flank until she was turning as he wanted. He leered at her protruding mound and high tits.

16

She responded well to commands, he thought, and silently thanked Sextus. Keeping her as one of his dogs had not ruined her. She was clearly beautiful and with a little discipline, compliance would come. It would be worth the effort, he thought. She was magnificent.

Just as the fort's other spirited animals—their dogs and horses—needed a firm hand, so did a savage beauty like this, he thought. The debate over "tame versus spirited" would never be over, but this animal clearly needed more discipline. He always enjoyed a little spirit, but open defiance, like she had shown him, was not acceptable.

He lowered the cane and stood to release the straps holding her elbows and wrists together. It was time. There was no rush, but he wanted to savor the feel of her trembling fingers on his skin. Rushing into these things like a pig in heat was a mistake, one he did not want to repeat. Her fear of the cane and now her fear of his cock had produced the most exquisite shudder. Rushing things now would destroy that sublime effect.

He pointed to his sandals and sat back in the chair as she untied and pulled them off. He watched as she worked, it would be exciting to bend her over the table while he caned her ass. He would penetrate her after her caning while she was still trembling with pain. The plan excited him.

She stood to remove his underwear and out of the corner of his eye he saw her ass twitching. Most men would have missed it, but Flaccus was not most men. He was an expert at interpreting body movements, and hers were clearly protesting the hook.

The hook-and-collar was his invention, a device he had created with the help of the camp's leather workers

17

and blacksmiths to increase the womanly curve in a young slave girl's back, to raise her ass, and to accustom her to anal penetration. At one end, was a high neck collar that forced her head up high; at the other was an iron ass hook that did the same for her ass. A locked chain, impossible for the slave to remove herself, connected the hook and the collar.

"Is the hook bothering you, dog-girl? Do you want me to remove it?"

She turned towards him but there was no sign of understanding in her dark eyes. He found the master key in his pouch and unlocked the chain then slowly, his hand on her bare hip, he pulled the hook out of her ass. She shuddered in sexual gratification and gratitude as the metal slipped out.

"I will need to put your hook-and-collar back on when we're done," he said unnecessarily then bent her over the table.

She did not resist. Sextus had beaten overt resistance out of her with his long whip. Like all Romans, the legate believed that slaves acted to avoid pain, that obedience was the result of pain, that corporal punishment and discipline turned minds towards compliance. He felt a touch of pride that the camp's sophisticated methods, many of which he had instituted, had produced such amazing creatures.

He flicked the cane between her legs to spread them then flicked lightly at the underside of her ass to get her up on her toes. Despite her earlier behavior, she was responding well to the touch of the wood, like a well-trained horse answering to the crop.

Every instinct in his body was screaming for him to ram his hard cock into her soft wet cunt, but he resisted.

He was a cat playing with his prey now. There was no escape for her now. He was her undisputed master...her god. She knew there was nothing ahead for her but pain and penetration. He felt a wave of immense power flow through his body.

This was the way their world worked, and she knew it.

He grabbed her long black hair, lifted her head, and stared into her eyes, savoring the look of total submission, then he ran his other hand down her backbone and between her ass cheeks to her anus and her clitoris. Stepping behind, he began to slowly massage her labia with his hand, slipping his finger inside occasionally.

Her quick breathing turned into a rapid sexual pant as he toyed with her. She wanted him now; she wanted him more than she had ever wanted anything. He knew the fear and her instinct for self-preservation was the cause of most of her arousal rather than any sexual attraction to him, but he was okay with that. In fact, her preferred it— the girl who fucked him out of fear was testifying to his immense power.

She was desperate to please him now, to win his favor. That was what counted. At this moment, he ruled over her like an emperor. He pulled her hair again until her body was upright, then twisted her nipple hard just because he could. Her cries of pain made his cock rock hard.

Don't rush things, you fool, he told himself! You have waited all day for this one...savor her in these final moments before...

He couldn't resist; he caned her again. She jerked in his grip and screamed the way he liked. The cane had found its mark on the sweet spot between her ass and her thighs. She writhed, begging him with her body to take her, to take all of her and...

Her movement excited him to cane her again. The plaintive cry of her total surrender aroused him like no one had done in a long time. He now understood why Sextus had kept her hidden. Unlike some of the stupid Britons they kept for auction, this one had the ability to excite a man's passions, to get him to do dangerous things. He pushed her down until she was kneeling between his legs.

"My cock wants to taste your sweet mouth before it plucks your flower," he said to himself.

A spittle of drool from the caning was running down her chin. Normally, he would not engage in fellatio without a ring gag, without tying the slave's arms tied back in a painful strappado, but it was different with this nymph. She had submitted fully to his dominance. Making a female slave writhe in your hands was an essential part of dominating her, especially with a Briton. It reoriented their primitive mind away from its natural tendency towards savagery.

The girl began to lick his scrotum then suck it into her mouth. After a time, she ran her tongue along the full length of his cock, teasing it to a joyously painful length.

She would be naked and unbound when she stepped onto the block, he thought, his mind wandering. His hook-and-collar, his fucking would make her more attractive. If she was lucky, one of the brothel owners would buy her. Life in their keeping would be easier—she could lie around during the day and suck men's cocks at night. It would be a much better life than being in a kitchen or being the handmaid of some rich woman. They whipped their girls out of jealousy, sometimes even disfiguring the truly beautiful ones to prevent them from outshining them. It was outrageous...a waste of a slave, but what could you expect? They were just women."

He felt wonderful as she swallowed him, taking him fully down her throat. How did a virgin learn such technique, he wondered? Her life as a slave could be a good one; all she needed to do was to obey, to comply, to submit as willingly as she was doing for him now. He put his hand behind her neck then held her head as her throat muscles massaged his cock while her tongue and lips reached out for his balls. It was as if she had been sucking cock all her life.

A natural cocksucker, he decided! He had known she would be special.

"Savor...the...taste...of it," he urged breathlessly as he pulled her head in closer, forgetting again that she could not speak Latin. "Your love of it will sustain you as a whore. Use your tongue to caress it. As it hardens, use your throat to massage the tip. Be gentle but firm, tight lipped. Most men will get excited at this point and try to fuck your mouth like it is your cunt. You will need to train yourself to deal with this instinct. Slow them down so that they can still fuck you the normal way—up your cunt and in your ass."

Ignoring his own unheard advice, he had already begun to ram it in and out, banging the cock head against the back of her throat with each thrust. Her grasping mouth felt too good for him to hold back. It was like a fur-lined glove, tight and smooth. She had achieved amazing suction and she had a way of moving her head that made it impossible for him to back out...a natural talent as a cocksucker.

He could come right now in her mouth then torment her for a while until he was potent again, maybe crop her feet. There would be plenty of time to break her hymen later, perhaps even to violate her asshole..."

"Slow down a little," he cautioned, more to himself than to her, "just use your tongue. Take my balls inside occasionally. I want to feel your lips on me...feel you worshipping my manhood. Harder, HARDER!"

He was banging the back of her throat viciously now, and he knew that ejaculation was only seconds away. He resigned himself to it and held back, working his way to a massive climax.

"Suck on it, suck on it, you Brit bitch," he groaned as his eyes rolled back.

Suddenly, he was spurting his semen in great globs into her mouth. Time seemed to stand still for him now; the massive orgasm had paralyzed him. Xara waited until his contraction was at its peak then she bit down hard and held on. Flaccus didn't scream exactly, his first sound was more like the surprised gasp of someone punched hard in the stomach. Xara held on as he screamed like a woman and fell to the ground jerking in pain and rolling, desperately trying to dislodge her. Blood was everywhere.

Xara release her teeth as the legate was still rolling, wailing in agony. She knew his shock would only last for another few seconds. For all his faults, Flaccus was a warrior and an experienced commander; he had a lifetime of experience dealing with surprises. Once he regained his mind, he would run outside for help, and she would not be able to stop him. It would be over then; the soldiers manning the wall would see him and raise the alarm. She leaped to her feet spitting his blood out of her mouth.

22

She stared down at Flaccus's writhing body, remembering how casually he had caned her, how the Romans had hacked her father to pieces and crucified her mother. Yes, her people had taught her that revenge was good, but it was the Romans who made it sweet. She raised her foot and brought her heel down hard on the commander's exposed larynx. His hands flew up to his throat forgetting the excruciating pain in his cock. He was struggling to breathe, and his lips were turning blue, but his fingers were working desperately to reshape his crushed airway.

She cocked her head and watched. Sextus's drunken disclosure that the legate would sell her immediately after her deflowering had convinced her that she had to act now. She had been patient, cowering as one of the dogs, waiting for the right time in a way that only a Briton could. Revenge, even it took generations, was part of her upbringing, her heritage.

Xara, now covered in blood, knelt beside him to watch him die, but that was not going to happen. Incredibly, his therapy was working: he was beginning to draw breath. He looked at her, terrified and pleading for his life, and she suddenly knew the truth—he was a false master, a pretender, a coward. He was afraid of death…afraid of her!

It was an epiphany. She had never imagined that her Roman masters knew fear. All the time she was with the dogs, she thought that their handlers were superior to her in every way. She considered her revenge to be that of a lesser being on a greater one. Suddenly, she knew it was all a lie—the Romans were just like her. Yes, they had better organization, better machines, better equipment, but they were no better.

"If you live, Legate," she said in Latin, "you will kill me. You will have no choice; I will die a horrible death on the cross like my mother did."

If she was lucky, she thought. Crucifixion was the punishment for a slave who struck a Roman master; she didn't know what the punishment was for a slave who killed her master. He was recovering quickly; in seconds, he would have the strength to push her aside and rush for the door.

Slowly, staring into his eyes, she lowered her raised knee onto his throat then pushed steadily enough to close the airway. He punched at her and scratched like a drowning, but she had strength and balance. When he began to convulse, bucking like a horse trying to throw its rider, she extended her free leg to maintain the pressure. His thrashing seemed to last for hours until, finally, the life went out of his eyes.

She felt nothing, only shame that she had once been the slave of a coward, that she had waited so long before challenging her roman captors. She stood up and fashioned his clothes into a rough covering. His heavy sandals were too big for her, but perhaps she could modify them. She shoved them into his pouch. It would be cold during the night, and she would need to keep warm if she was to make it as far as the Great Northern Forest. Even if she did reach the forest, the Atrebates ruled the forest and killed all trespassers.

First things first, she thought, escape the Romans and their cross then worry about the Atrebates. Suddenly, the air trapped in the legate's lungs gurgled up in a bloody froth. She jumped back, startled, then felt ashamed.

This was not the time for fear; this was what her father would have said. She was free now and would never surrender to anyone especially to another Roman ever again. She lifted the legate's *gladius* then threw it on top of his body. It was far too heavy for her, but his thin knife felt just right. The sword was a man's weapon; she would make her mark with this sharp knife. Her eyes fell on the hook-and-collar laying in the corner and stared at it for a long time. He thought I enjoyed having his iron cock up my ass. Were all Romans this stupid in matters of sex, she wondered? She filed the though away for later.

She stepped closer to the corpse of Lucius Flaccus. Kneeling, she dipped her finger in the pool of blood near his torn cock then wrote the Latin word *ignavus*, coward, on his hairy chest. She knew the message would enrage his men, push them to hunt harder for her, but their urgency to nail her to a cross would also cause them to make mistakes. This was another thing her father had taught her—remain calm in the face of your enemy's excitement.

She knew this was, at least in part, a rationalization for desecrating him. What she mostly wanted was to declare her private war on the Romans, to let them know that she was not afraid, that she knew they were vulnerable and that they were…

Coward was a fitting epitaph for a man like Lucius Flaccus, she thought.

She waited until dark then slipped out of the guardhouse and began to run through the field. She had the strength of her ancestors in her, but it was unlikely that she could outrun the legion's cavalry in her race to the forest, but it did not didn't bother her. She would be satisfied if she could take another Roman or two to the grave with her before she killed herself. She knew that no specific number of Roman lives would quench her thirst for revenge, but each one she took would help.

Chapter Two – Caratacus

Caratacus watched the Romans rush from Rumabo's gates. There was a full cohort of men in the infantry column, at least four hundred men, and almost a full *alae* (wing) of cavalry, another one hundred men and horses. What was so important that they would send out five hundred men?

His men had seen a slave escape the night before, a girl, but it was not reasonable that they would send out so many in search of one escaped slave unless... Was it possible, had the slave killed one of their legionaries. It still didn't make any sense—perhaps they would send out a *centuria* (eighty men) or even two, but a full cohort...for a girl?

He crept away from his hiding place and joined a string of his men in a small culvert.

"The Romans are out of Rumabo...in force," he told them. "I cannot see any reason for it."

"Should we prepare an ambush, Lord?" one of the younger warriors asked.

Caratacus didn't answer for a long time. The Catuvellauni were in a life and death struggle with the Romans, who saw them as slaves. This mostly meant lethal harassment and quick strikes to steal supplies and weapons. An ambush was a major engagement, typically in the open where the Romans had the advantage of superior organization, training, leadership, and equipment.

"No, we will not provoke a force of this size unless they come close to a village."

He was staring directly at the man who had spoken.

"I want them watched carefully, and I want our men to keep track of the slave, the girl who escaped."

The tribe did not normally accept strangers, they killed them—it was a matter of security—but something was amiss here, and he had a feeling that the slave girl was somehow involved. As chief of the Catuvellauni, it was his responsibility to find out what it was. He was also curious, if a slave girl had done something for the fort's commander to activate five hundred Romans, he wanted to know what it was, and he wanted to meet her.

***

The Romans were better trackers than Xara had expected.

They used their dogs and horses skillfully and they were patient—methodically dividing the search area into neat blocks and meticulously isolating and searching each block. Her attempt to incite them into making foolish mistakes had not worked—apparently Lucius Flaccus was not as beloved as she thought. It didn't matter, she had known from the beginning that reaching the forest was unlikely.

Slowly, inexorably, no matter what evasive tactic she tried, the Roman net continued to close tighter and tighter around her. After a few days, they had her trapped in a large thicket still miles from the relative safety of the forest with all possible paths to the forest blocked. She knew it was over for her.

She was pleased though with the way things had turned out. She had evaded what seemed to be hundreds of soldiers for three days and even managed to kill one of the Roman's Germanic mercenaries with her dagger. The man had ventured far from his companions, so she was able to leap out of the grass and slit his throat without him setting off an alarm. He had been surprised, and because of it, his reaction time was fatally slow.

It was a valuable lesson for her—he had underestimated her, and this had caused his surprise and his death. It was a valuable insight, one that it was unlikely she would ever get to use it again. It was also disappointing. She wanted to kill Romans not Germans, and more than one. However, after finding the dead German, the searchers had tightened their defenses. Getting close enough to cut another soldier without them catching her was now highly unlikely.

She stared off into the distance in the direction of the Great Northern Forest. It would have been good to live longer and killed more Romans, but she had done what she could. At least she had taken the life of Lucius Flaccus. He had been a patrician and even though in the end he had behaved like a coward, he was a legate, the commander of a Roman legion. How many others could make such a claim? Killing a coward, of course, did not have the same value as killing a courageous warrior, but the Romans had not given her the opportunity to kill more of their men.

She would have enjoyed killing Sextus, the torturer, as well. Not that he was as bad as Lucius Flaccus—his sadism was a requirement for the legion's chief torturer—but killing Sextus would have evened the scales. It would have been good to report to her mother that she had killed her torturer; she would have liked avenging avenge all the Britons he had tortured.

Britons...

She was a Taexali not a Briton. In their never-ending arrogance, the Romans referred to all members of the native tribes as Celts or Brits even though many were not Celtic or British. Her people had lived on this land long before the Celts came. Devana, the Taexali village the invading Romans had destroyed, her village, had existed since the beginning of time. Now both her village and the Taexali people were gone. She might be the last of them.

It was unfortunate she could not live to tell the story of her people. She could not risk the Romans taking her alive. They had nets for taking slaves alive; if they caught her in one of them, she would be helpless, unable to fight them or to take her life. They would strip her and nail her wrists and ankles to a cross. She had seen how other women and men died on the cross, how they suffered for hours, sometimes for days, how their screams and pleas for mercy shamed them and their people. She could not, would not allow this to happen to her. If she truly was the last of the Taexali, it was her duty to die honorably.

Huddling deeper in the underbrush, she ran her finger along the knife's edge. It was a good blade; she would give them this, the Romans made good weapons. She moved the knife's point to the bottom of her rib cage just below her heart and took a deep breath. This was the only way she could escape them now.

She heard a pack of dogs baying in the distance. They were close now, too close to delay any longer. The sound of the dogs will be my death song, she thought wryly, remembering her time with Sextus's mastiffs. She would slip the knife carefully inside her chest until it found her heart them pull up hard to ensure that the wound was fatal. She would need to endure the pain to be sure the wound was fatal; she could not hesitate or falter,

What waited for her after death, she wondered…eternal darkness…the afterlife? It didn't matter, now that death was her only choice, now that…

DO IT, DO IT NOW…a voice screamed in her head. Only a coward hesitates! She looked up at the sky saddened by the thought of leaving this life, then she closed her eyes and…

The sudden sound of something flying at her made her turn her eyes, but she wasn't fast enough to see the club thrown at her head. There was a flash of white light then nothing. Later, she learned that Caratacus had launched the club from thirty feet away, knocking her unconscious.

***

Caratacus stared at the girl. The club had put a gash in her head and her blood was spilling onto the ground. He ripped off a piece of cloth and tied it around her head to stop the bleeding. The roman's dogs could follow a good blood trail for miles. She wasn't Catuvellauni, perhaps Votadini or Taexali, but it didn't matter; anyone not of the Catuvellauni he would normally take as a slave or kill. She was too beautiful to kill.

He tested the firmness of her breasts then stripped off her loincloth and sandals. Catuvellauni slaves went naked until their master awarded them cloth. She was tall but slim with firm tits and an exciting, sexual shape. She was a fine prize, but he still had no idea why the Romans were after her with such ferocious intent. How could such a thin girl hurt them so badly that…

The sound of dogs baying rousted him from his thoughts. They needed to hide. He hoisted her over his shoulder and waded into the water then carried her for half-a-mile until he found a small rivulet off to the side and followed it for several hundred yards. He lifted the cover of the camouflaged pit and dumped her inside then masked their lingering scent with the carcass of a dead racoon he had killed earlier.

He climbed in after her and pulled the cover over them.

***

Xara regained conscious slowly. She was in a hole, with a dirty cloth shoved in her mouth, her hands bound behind, and the unmistakable feel of a man's body pressing hard against hers. She opened her eyes and saw nothing but darkness. Had they buried her with a corpse, ALIVE? She tried to yell and managed a desperate grunt then felt impossible strong hands on her neck, blocking her air.

He wasn't trying to kill her, he wanted her to remain quiet. Slowly, he relaxed his grip and she breathed, but remained silent.

"There are Roman's outside. If you make a sound, it will be your last," a voice whispered in her ear, pressing a knife against her throat. She was a hideaway, a hunting blind, a hole in the ground covered by grass and bushes that hunters used to conceal themselves.

"I am Caratacus, chief of the Catuvellauni, and you are now my slave."

She was no one's slave, she thought, not ever again, but knew that this was not the time to debate the point. The Roman's searching outside had no interest in enslaving her; they wanted her dead, crucified. He said he was Caratacus, chief of the Catuvellauni. She knew of Caratacus, but why would the chief of the Catuvellauni be in a thicket. Had he been hunting...? His body against hers felt like Roman steel wrapped in skin. She would have no chance against him this close.

After a time, she felt him relax. The romans had moved on...they were safe. Suddenly, she felt his knee between her legs then his legs holding hers open. He was on top of her, his hand reaching down to spread her labia. At once, he was inside, his cock was inside and pressing against...

The pain of his cock tearing her hymen was terrible, but she didn't have time to think about it. He was inside her...HE WAS INSIDE HER, ramming his cock into her vagina with the raging intensity of a wild animal in heat. She could not process the feelings, the mixture of pain and...pleasure was something so alien that... the orgasm was so sudden, so violent in its contraction that her entire body stiffened then relaxed. She lost consciousness for a moment then awoke to him grunting and ramming. His climax seemed equally intense.

He lay there for a long time refusing to pull out, waiting for his enormous erection to dissolve of its own accord. In the darkest hour of the night, he pulled her out of the hole, washed her bound body in the nearby stream, put her over his shoulder and ran. She could feel his muscles moving, feel his hand on her ass, her tits bouncing on his bare back.

At one point, he stopped and put her gently on the ground to prevent her making any sound then waited. A pair of legionaries, clearly outliers assigned to the periphery of the search area to catch anyone who slipped through the search line walked into the tiny clearing unaware of their presence.

Caratacus remained still until they were close then he rose like a ghost and slit both of their throats with the stolen gladius he kept at his waist. Xara watched in disbelief; his movement was so quick and deadly silent that it reminded her of the dogs the Romans had put her with—they were also quick and silent killers.

After another few miles, he put her down, retied her hands in front, and used a cord he had taken off one of the Romans to fashion a tether.

***

The next morning, she woke in a warm hut, smoky with the flame of a cooking fire. A woman with Catuvellauni tribal markings on her face was washing the blood from her hair.

"Shhh," she whispered. "I am Liosa. You are in the hut of Caratacus, chief of the Catuvellauni. He is our master, and we are his slaves."

"I am no one's slave," Xara whispered, still a little unsteady from the head blow.

"Caratacus took you out of the marsh; he stole you from the Romans, this makes him your master."

Caratacus...?

Xara closed her eyes. Her head felt dizzy as if it was going to fall off and she was nauseous. The wild Celtic tribes did not welcome strangers, but the ongoing fight against the Roman's had changed things, which was why she was still alive. The ancient feuds between the tribes now seemed trivial compared to the existential threat posed by the Roman invaders.

34

Caratacus…the chief of the Catuvellauni had rescued her…fucked her? Why…? Why had he taken her from the thicket and brought her here, to one of their villages. Did the Catuvellauni need slaves so badly?

They will try to make me a slave, she thought, but I will not allow this to happen. I have sworn to die as a warrior avenging my family and there was no turning away from that oath now. She looked around for the exit and for a weapon.

"The Master has posted guards outside," Liosa whispered fearfully guessing what was in her mind. "They have need of slaves because so many have died in the fight against the Romans, but if you try to escape, they will kill you. You should do as you are told."

Xara lay back on the rough cot and remained still as the slave Liosa cleaned her wound. It wasn't fear of the warriors killing her that made her relax, it was the fact that the Catuvellauni were engaged in fighting the Romans. This was all she, Xara, the last of the Taexali, lived for now.

***

Caratacus sat cross-legged facing her over the fire. He was a fierce and imposing figure, heavily muscled and more than six feet tall, with flowing hair and a great mustache that fell down the side of his face like two sharp fangs. Xara sat on her haunches dressed in a loincloth and a halter made of animal hide. Her hands were on her knees in a slave position as Liosa had explained the Master would expect.

"What is your name, girl? Who are your people?"

"Xara of the Taexali."

35

He blinked, but there was no other indication of surprise.

"The Taexali no longer exist except as Roman slaves," he said quietly.

"I exist and I am not a slave."

Caratacus waited for her to say something more, but Xara remained silent. Her time with the dogs had taught her the value of listening.

"You are wrong. I saved your life and took you from the Romans. You are my slave by right of conquest."

"I am no one's slave."

Caratacus blinked again. No one ever spoke to him like this. If Xara had been a man, he would have killed him. Instead, he smiled, curious.

"The Taexali fought bravely at Devana. Our spies reported thousands of dead, and a hundred Roman crosses after the fight. The Romans only nail their enemies to the crosses when they are badly hurt. We consider crosses a sign of great honor for warriors."

She didn't say anything. She remembered watching the romans mob and butcher her father then watching her mother suffocate slowly for a full day on one of those crosses. There was no honor in it, only suffering and an ugly death.

"Is that where they took you as a slave…at Devana?"

"Yes."

"Why were the Romans hunting you, a slave girl, with such a large force? We have seen their cavalry combing the area for days. Why were you so important to them?"

Xara hesitated. This man was not a Roman and he had saved her life, but her mother had taught her to avoid those from other tribes, to be wary of their intentions.

36

"I escaped."

"That was brave," he said impatiently, "but the legion's commander at Rumabo would not send a cohort of infantry and an *alae* of cavalry after a single slave. He would send a handful of horsemen and dogs. The Romans are fanatics about catching escaped slaves, but even they are not so foolish as to waste that many legionaries to chase a slave girl, even one as beautiful as you, Xara of the Taexali.

"Now tell me the truth," he said in a threatening tone, "or I will have you whipped and give you to my men. Many of them have already asked my permission to fuck you."

"As you did, Chief?" she asked, her hand moving towards the spot on her waist where Lucius Flaccus's dagger had hung. Roman or not, no man was ever going to enslave her again, not while she had the means to prevent it. Caratacus eyes followed her hand.

"Is this what you are looking for, slave? You know, we burn slaves who threaten their Masters…cook them on a spit over a low flame. Is that what you want?"

He pulled Lucius Flaccus's dagger out from under a rug.

"Do you want a slave's death?"

Zara stared at him then placed her hand back on her leg.

"To escape, I had to kill the *legatus legionis,* Lucius Flaccus."

"You killed the legate, the commander of the slave depot at Rumabo Imperium…?" he asked skeptically.

"Yes."

"…And that's why they wanted you so badly?"

"Yes."

His face clouded over. Lying to a master earned a slave the same death as threatening him.

"How did you kill him...?"

"I...I found a way to distract him by damaging a body part then, while he cried about it, I crushed his throat."

It didn't feel right telling another man, any man, that she had bitten another man's prick with her teeth. Caratacus just stared, still skeptical.

"...And this is his knife, the legate's knife?"

"Yes."

He stared at it, especially at the silver eagle embossed in its ebony hilt. A silver eagle with its claws extended was the traditional symbol of a commander.

Xara's eyes fell on the knife. Was she fast enough to wrest it from his grip? Not likely, she decided. Without the knife she had no way to defend herself or to kill herself. Without it, he might succeed in making her his slave. Suddenly, she remembered the taste and feel of Flaccus's cock in her mouth. She did not have a knife when she did that to him. Then again, Flaccus had been a coward and Caratacus was anything but a coward.

He saw her eyes on the weapon and the look of fierce determination on her face. Suddenly, he knew she was telling the truth. He sheathed the dagger and handed it back to her.

"I could have left you for the Romans, Xara of the Taexali. I don't need another slave even one as beautiful as you, badly enough to stand alone against a Roman cohort. I saved you because anyone who can evade the bastards for three days then kill herself to avoid capture deserves my attention. Are you willing to fight with us?"

He waited for her answer. Xara had never considered joining with anyone in her fight against the Romans. This was a personal vendetta for her, an act of political vengeance. She had little interest in the politics of the Roman invasion except as it affected her and her people.

He raised his eyebrows, and she knew he would not ask again. If she was not a slave, then she was an enemy. She knew that joining him put her on a different path, but she also had an instinct that trusting him was the right thing to do. She nodded then lowered her head in the universal symbol of submission. She would join his fight and subject herself to his orders.

"Good. Did the Roman commander die well…?"

She looked up. It was obvious that Caratacus expected her to say that he did. He was after all a man; he had proven that with his cock in the blind. He also needed to think that the man he fought was a great warrior, it would diminish him to think anything else.

"He was in pain, but he died as a warrior should…silently," she lied.

Caratacus smiled. There was no reason for her to tell him that the Roman had died a coward, begging for her, a slave, to have mercy on him.

"The Romans are cruel, but they fight well; they are worthy adversaries," he said, confirming her suspicion.

She stayed quiet. The Romans were vermin, she thought—devils from some evil place in the south—but he needed to believe they were "worthy adversaries."

"How can I reward you for, ah, killing a leader of our enemy, Xara of the Taexali?"

She didn't hesitate.

"Teach me how to kill Romans, my lord," she said simply. "I have a knife, but I am not yet well-trained in its use."

He nodded.

"And…"

"Make me your woman…for a time," she whispered. "This was the Roman commander's intent, but he never got to finish the job. I would rather have a Catuvellauni warrior as a lover than some Roman pig. I have come to appreciate your…manhood."

He stared at her for a moment then rose and walked to the door where he dismissed the two guards waiting outside. In a moment he had stripped off his pants. Xara stared at his cock. It was flaccid but still huge with at least twice the girth of Flaccus's slim member. She stood in front of him and slipped out of the clothes Liosa had given her. Without thinking, she knelt before him then put her face near his cock. Her brief time with Flaccus had left her with the impression that coitus started with fellatio. Having asked for his sexual attention, she was ready to suck his cock to get it hard, but before she could latch onto it with her lips, Caratacus lifted her to her feet.

"Another time, minx, when we know more about each other. I have no desire to test your promise of loyalty with my manhood."

She turned toward him confused and he smiled.

"Never," he whispered, "repeat your story about the legate to another man, Xara. The manner of Lucius Flaccus's death, even for a Roman, was…regrettable. He was a brave warrior. Other men will not understand the fire that beats in our hearts to destroy Romans with such, with any…means. Do you understand?"

Instead of answering, she reached down and began to massage his balls then to stroke his cock. In seconds he was hard. She pushed him down on the furs then lifted her leg over his and descended. Her labia was open and wet, and he slipped his cock head inside sensing her tightness.

Caratacus stared into her eyes, she was ready. He put his hands on the back of her shoulders.

"Death to all Romans," he whispered hoarsely.

"Death to all Romans," she repeated, closing her eyes.

He pulled down hard on her shoulder and she threw her head back and moaned. He fucked her, bellowing like a bull then turned her on her back and fucked her with wild abandon. She could feel the pleasure through the pain, and she began to move with him, contracting her muscles instinctually to induce the deepest possible penetration and the largest possible climax. They came in a fury of moving bodies and fluids as they had in the hole. She had never known, never even guessed that such pleasure existed. Now she knew.

Caratacus, who was already married with children, invested her as his concubine. During the day, and true to his word, he taught her how to fight and how to wage war.

***

Xara trained with the Catuvellauni for six months. At night, she slept in Caratacus's bed where they fucked like rabbits. When they weren't fucking, they talked. Xara had a quick mind and an insider's view of the Romans. Caratacus found it useful to talk to her about them.

41

"We have been waging guerilla war against the Romans for years," he told her, "...but this phase of the battle is nearing its end. We don't have the means to feed our people if we continue to strike and run. We must fight them soon; we must meet them in the open and defeat their legions in battle."

"Can you do that, Lord?" she said quietly, rubbing her nipples on the side of his massive chest as she stroked his now-limp cock.

"Of course," he said confidently. "The Romans have their forts and their stockade encampments, but to take land, to take slaves, they must come out and face us. When they do, we will annihilate them."

"...And they will send more soldiers," she said quietly.

"...until they get tired of losing men," he countered.

"They have never lost a war,"

"How do you know that?"

"I secretly learned their language and I listened when they talked. No one paid any attention to me. They found it amusing to tie me with their dogs."

"That was just soldier's talk, Xara. They don't really know anything. You don't think their leaders tell them when they lose a war."

She didn't answer. She had heard them talking about wars in far off places and there was plenty of talk about battles lost, but no one ever mentioned that Rome was losing a war...anywhere. It took a while, but eventually she acquired a more complete insight into the Roman character. They were like ants—insidious and industrious. They had setbacks, but they never gave up, they never failed to push forward, not until they had defeated their enemy. The conclusion that Rome was unstoppable was

42

not just soldierly gossip or Roman pride; the men talked as if it were an undeniable fact, and she believed them.

"Perhaps you can negotiate a peace with them, Lord…?"

He was quiet for a long time.

"They have no interest in peace, Xara. They want land and slaves. The choice for us is simple—give up our land and become Roman slaves or fight. Isn't that the same choice you faced?"

"Yes, Lord."

She could tell that he was finished talking about Romans. What more was there to say?

"Shall I use my mouth tonight, Lord?"

She could feel him stiffen. Her strong, lean body and her haunting face, especially her dark flashing eyes, made her easy to love. The one thing he still would not allow, however, was cocksucking, what the Romans called fellatio. Her story about how she had gotten the best of Lucius Flaccus had settled in his mind and festered.

"Are you afraid of me, my lord?" she asked playfully.

"A king is not afraid of anything or anyone…"

"I yearn for the taste of you, Master, for the feel of your powerful cock in my mouth, but you deny me that pleasure and you are wrong to do so. You are not a Roman pig; I would never hurt you…that way. I worship your cock."

"I know it, my little she-wolf…in my head I know it, but my cock is still…hesitant. It whispers, 'once a biter, always a biter' and those words echo in my head like…"

She reached down and playfully squeezed his scrotum. She knew he would never be free of this phobia.

She needed to take the chance that he would reject her again.

"Your fear is irrational, my Lord. Whip me if you will, but I must have my fill of you."

She lowered her head into his lap and gently kissed the tip of his cock then licked off the pre-ejaculate that had collected there. It tasted salty. She moved to the base of his cock and licked his scrotum; she could feel his hand on the back of her neck. He could snap it in a second—a painful second for him to be sure—but she would be dead.

She sucked one ball into her mouth and masticated it with her tongue and lips, careful not to touch it with her teeth. Then, while he was moaning, she sucked in the other and used her cheeks to help. She could feel them swelling, feel his cock stiffening to battle length. Without regard for his reaction, she changed position and sucked his penis inside. It filled her as Flaccus's member never had. It wasn't just big, which it was, it was the man to whom it belonged. He was a giant, a hero, and sucking hero cock was a privilege, an honor...

Slowly, he grabbed her hair and pulled her off.

"That's enough for tonight, my minx. Tomorrow we will do more."

She thought they were done, but instead he grunted, turned her over onto her stomach, and roughly spread her legs open. With a growing frenzy, he scooped a dollop of grease from a nearby jar and put it between her ass cheeks, into her asshole. She knew what was coming and shuddered in anticipation. Having Caratacus's enormous cock up her ass was both a joy and a terror.

44

"I am content for now with those holes of yours that don't have teeth," he whispered as he reamed her anus with his finger.

He put his cock against her asshole and slowly pushed his way past her sphincter then paused. She moaned with the sweet pain of it—his prick was long and thick. Instinctively, she squeezed her ass cheeks and managed to catch a part of his dangling scrotum then she squeezed harder, compressing the sack, and pressing on his balls. He groaned with the feel of it then began to fuck her vigorously. Her sphincter muscles responded with equal fury, acting like vaginal muscles on steroids.

She had no choice. He was incredibly strong, and she was helpless in his hands, impaled on his hard member. Suddenly he moved his hands to her front and gripping her tits as if they were the reins of a wild horse. The stabilization they brought proved necessary as he began to ram it inside with an intensity she had never known. She came when he came in a furious flurry of contractions so powerful they shook her body from head to toe. The violence of his orgasm was no less severe. It was a long time before their contractions subsided before they were sane enough to consider separating.

The next morning, Xara got up and left before he awoke. She was waiting in the glen when her trainer arrived. Caratacus had kept his word about teaching her the fine points of single combat.

She was fast and agile and an excellent student. In a few weeks, she was regularly beating the warriors assigned to teach the Catuvellauni women how to fight, but despite her ability, no one would assign her to the men's training. It finally took the chief to order his best fighters to work with her. Much to their chagrin, she quickly managed to push them to their limits. It was only when he assigned the tribe's best warriors, the members of his personal guard, that she began to see the limits of her abilities, and to learn the true art of killing.

It was during one of these sessions, that word came that a Roman legion, the Second, Augustus's own, was moving north in their direction. Caratacus summoned his war council and prepared to meet them. It was the first time an entire legion had ventured this far north.

"If we can inflict enough damage on it in open battle, we can then use guerilla tactics to snap at their flanks during their long march back to safety. We can destroy the entire legion this way, and once we have destroyed one of their legions, they will have to beg us for peace. It is too good an opportunity to miss."

He decided that the valley known as Wolf's Glen would be an excellent place for an ambush and he sent word that all the Catuvellauni—men, women, slaves, and even children—would participate in "the battle to end the war."

Xara felt suddenly sad. She knew that even the destruction of a full legion would not deter the Romans— they would just send another legion until they had pacified the Catuvellauni—but she said nothing. Caratacus had no choice and neither did she, nor did he have any choice but to order her to fight with the women; his men would not tolerate a woman in their midst. She knew he was secretly glad, fighting with the women gave her a better opportunity to survive. There was no arguing this with him now, he had made his decision.

"Thank you, Lord," she whispered in his ear the night before the battle. They had just finished having sex,

46

amazing sex, and he was still inside. "I will not shame you on the battlefield."

He reached down with both hands feeling her body then rested them on ass cheeks. It was as if he were trying to lock her shape into his mind.

"Remember why we fight, Xara of the Taexali. Remember that we will win one day…"

Chapter Three – Wolf's Glen

Wolf's Glen was a valley with a serpentine trail at the bottom and steep hills on either side. Caratacus knew that the Romans would need to narrow and lengthen their column to pass through and that they would post scouts on the hilltops to prevent ambush.

"The key to our success," he reminded the captains around him, "…is the scouts. We must capture them and force them to reveal the signal for 'all clear.' Once we have it, our men, dressed as Romans, will give the signal from the hilltops. If we fail with this, the Romans will reform for defense, and we will fail."

Xara, standing in the back, knew exactly what he was thinking. Caratacus had twelve thousand Catuvellauni fighters to put against the legion's four-thousand eight-hundred infantrymen and one-hundred and twenty cavalrymen—an advantage of more than two to one. The Romans, however, were well-trained and well-disciplined; they knew the latest, most effective battle tactics; and most importantly, they had combat experience from a thousand fights in Macedonia, Syria, Judea, and Spain. The Second Legion, the Augusta Legion, was one of the empire's most combat-ready and feared units. The advantage in numbers would disappear quickly if the battlefield initiative shifted to the Romans.

His plan-of-attack was simple—a medium-sized group of Catuvellauni fighters would split he column in two then hold back reinforcements from the rear. A small force would then charge down the western slope and engage the front in a diversionary attack; when the legionaries from the front turned to meet the attackers, the main Catuvellauni force would charge down the eastern slope and attack them from the rear.

It was a good plan, Zara thought, one that made the most of his advantages. It was also simple, which she knew instinctively was necessary for his untrained force. The only question in her mind was whether the Roman commander, Legate Senatorus Plecio, and his military advisor, Prefect Gaius Lepidi, would turn the front of the column to meet the diversionary attack from the western slope. She had her doubts. After hours of listening to the soldiers of the Ninth Legion talk about battles, she knew that the Romans and their commanders, especially their military commanders—the prefect and the centurions—were professionals. Could Caratacus fool them? Could his advantage of surprise and terrain overcome the battle-hardened Augustus Legion?

"I would rather be with the men in the east. That's where the real fight will occur," Xara had told Caratacus as he was dressing for battle.

"You will fight on the western slope as I ordered," he replied quietly.

"I can help. I want to fight with the men."

He grabbed her by the neck and pushed her against a post. She couldn't speak.

"You will do as I order, Xara. The diversion from the west is an important part of my battle plan. Your ferocity will set an example. Once our women see how one of the Taexali people fight, they will take heart."

She stared into his eyes and knew there was more to his decision than inspiration. He wanted her to live and was assigning her to the diversionary force because that was where she had the best chance of survival. He put her down and turned away.

"You owe me a debt, Xara," he said with his back turned. "You can repay it by following my order and rallying the women."

He walked to the door then turned and spoke.

"If the Roman commander turns his men to meet the western attack, we will win," he said quietly, "if not, we will lose. Yes, I want you to live, but I also need you in the west to show the others what real courage is like. Once our enemy sees the damage a wisp of a girl like you does to their ranks, they will turn. I know it."

She could see the truth in what he was saying.

"Stay safe, my Lord," she said.

He nodded then turned and walked out.

***

Centurion Marcus Metella, responsible for the 2nd Century of the 4th Cohort, watched the scout on the hilltop give the proper signal that the slopes were clear. The man was too far away to make out his features, but the way he waved the flag was correct…everything was correct. Still, a vague sense of disquiet had settled in his chest. A sense he had learned in twenty years of battle not to ignore.

"Tighten the ranks, Viper," he growled to his number two, *Principales Optio* (sergeant) Spurius Vipsanius. "I want the men alert and ready to follow orders."

"Yes, Centurion."

Viper turned away and walked up and down the ranks of the eighty men of the 2nd Century muttering a warning. It wasn't important what he said or what the Centurion said, what was important was that they know that the Centurion was on edge. His instincts had saved their lives dozens of times.

Metella scanned the hills again and watched as other far-off scouts gave the right signal. He glanced ahead at the prefect's back. The old man was nervous as well, Metella could see it in the way he sat in his saddle, in the stiffness of his back. Neither of them liked having the legion march in the two lines required by the width of the trail. It meant that the back of the column was more than a mile from the front. Too far to run quickly if the savages attacked.

He shook his head. Maybe his instincts were wrong this time. The scouts had all signaled that the hills were clear...maybe he was just jumpy, maybe he had been in too many fights, lost too many friends. He glanced up ahead again and saw Prefect Lepidi stand in his stirrups, scanning for danger. Maybe he and Lepidi needed a rest.

***

Xara screamed as she rushed down the hill at the Roman line with two thousand Catuvellauni women. The fear she had felt earlier was gone; in its place was an unquenchable rage that she was finally getting to expel. She was now free to wreak havoc on her hated enemy. It was a glorious release of all the poison she had been holding inside.

She could see their faces now and they looked like Lucius Flaccus, and Sextus, and the men of his torture detachment. Somewhere in that small part of her mind that was still rational, she knew this could not be true— Flaccus was dead, and the Ninth Legion was still in Rumabo—but she didn't stop to argue with herself. She

51

knew she would fight harder if she thought she was fighting Sextus and his men.

She heard someone shout an order and the two lines of soldiers turned as one man. She could see the two other lines of Roman's behind moving to the right of the first two lines forming an in-depth defensive phalanx of four lines.

She glanced quickly to her side. Liosa, the slave girl who had cleaned her wounds when she first came to the Catuvellauni was leaping over the Roman shields like a demon from Hell. She grabbed a soldier's helmet in flight and broke his neck with her momentum. A man in the second line struck out with his spear and impaled her on it as she fell. The girl had been Caratacus's lover before she came to the tribe. Instead of crashing into the Romans, Xara stopped and turned sideways to avoid the spears and swords poking out from between the shields.

Only the left two lines had turned to face them, the two lines to the right were still facing forward. Xara knew that the women's attack needed to turn the other lines so the main attack would come at the roman's back. The outcome of the battle hinged on the commander giving the order for the lines to turn into the fight.

One of the Romans near her moved his shield to the side to thrust at her, but he was far too slow. She twisted away from the point as she reached out and slashed at his now-exposed neck. A fountain of hot blood sprayed over her as she turned to sever the femoral artery of the soldier on her right.

It was all about speed now, speed, strength, and courage. She could hear the behind her slamming into the Roman line, screaming like demons from Hell. Most of them ran directly into the Roman's spears and swords, impaling themselves, but some managed to dislodge the shields so that those that followed could take advantage of the openings and fall on the spearmen in the second line.

Suddenly, there was a break in the lines near her, exposing the men still facing forward in the third and fourth lines. Xara's heart leaped in her chest. *They were doing it!* There was panic in the third line as their comrades fell to the onslaught unable to defend themselves. Several, not waiting for orders, turned in panic to meet the women's charge. She could hear centurions shouting orders, cursing those who had turned.

A spearman in the third line, seeing two of his friends dead at her feet, lunged at her with his spear but he was also too slow. Xara twisted her body to the side at the hips and slid her knife down his spear shaft to cut into the man's exposed hands. The tactic wounded but did not stop him. In a move too fast to see, she slipped the knife effortlessly into the fatal space between his helmet and his breastplate. He stared at her, surprised that he could not open his mouth—her thin blade had pinned his jaw closed. She pushed again until she reached his brain then withdrew the blade.

The *decanus* (corporal) in charge of this part of the line watched in horror as a hundred women killed thirty of his men in as many seconds. The wildcats were now fully in their midst. Still, there was no command to turn the right-hand lines. Only those legionaries immediately threatened had turned to fight. The prefect was giving the Catuvellauni women the opportunity to kill his men rather than turn them to a defensive position.

Xara saw what was happening and rushed forward into the center. The corporal saw this and shouted an order to engage her. Immediately, two legionaries stepped forward and squared off on her, their spears lowered, as the fighting raged around them. The well-disciplined legionaries still had not broken formation, but all heads had turned towards her contest with the two spearmen, The corporal knew he needed to stop her. The slim girl and her flashing blade was creating panic among his men and inspiring the Catuvellauni women to fight harder.

The soldier to Xara's front dropped his spear, drew his *gladius*, and smiled evilly at her, daring her to turn away from him. The second man stepped cautiously to her side keeping her at bay with his spear's tip. The men in the lines took a step back to give their comrades room to complete the deadly maneuver. Xara knew instinctively that once the second man had flanked her, she would be as good as dead. As much as she hated them, she knew the Romans were good fighters. The only way to beat them was to disrupt their process, to surprise them in a way they did not expect.

She dived for the grinning man's legs with blinding speed, slashing as she fell. Miraculously, her knife connected, severing the tendons on the side of his knee. He crashed down like a wounded buffalo. The second man tried to jump over his friend's body and pin her to the ground with his spear, but instead of rolling away as he expected, Xara rolled towards him, cancelling the advantage of his long spear. Before he could reposition his weapon, she had slipped her knife past his balls and into his abdomen then with a quick pull of her wrist, she eviscerated him.

He roared in pain staring at his unraveling intestines then sat down on his wailing companion, pinning him to the ground. Xara struck out again with her knife and penetrated the wailing man's brain through his eye socket.

She spined away, pulling herself out of the bloody puddle then stared back, challenging the gawking men to fight her. One of them bellowed, lowered his sword, and charged at her like a knight on a horse. She stepped to the side at the last moment and sliced the side of his neck as he rushed past leaving a trail of red blood on the glen's green grass.

A circle formed around her as more men stepped forward to fight. Outside the circle, she could see screaming men and women, flailing bodies, and separated body parts littering the ground. No one stepped forward to engage her. Panting, still wild with rage, she glanced at the Roman column outside her immediate area. Incredibly, despite massive carnage, the Roman commander still had not turned his men.

The corporal stepped forward with disbelief and disgust on his face. How could a savage, a slender girl, defeat six of his best men in combat? Suddenly, he unfurled a net and threw it over her. She slashed at it and managed to free her blade, but other men were already on her. She waited for his gladius to slice into her neck, but instead of putting the sharp steel against her skin, he drove the hilt of his sword into her skull just under her ear, stunning her. It wasn't a fatal blow; that would have been merciful; he wanted her to suffer for what she had done. Quickly, he ordered a man to bind her in a hogtie.

On the hilltop, Caratacus watched the women engage. He had not expected them to win, but he did think the Roman prefect, the column's military advisor, would have turned more troops into defensive positions against them. Unfortunately, the Roman was not rising to the bait. He was watching, waiting patiently for the main attack while hundreds of his men died. Caratacus reluctantly ordered the main attack to begin. He could not wait any longer; the legion's rear might break through any second to reinforce the front.

As soon as the first warriors stepped over the hillcrest, the prefect advised the commander to turn the two right lines towards the attack and assume defensive positions. A Roman trumpet sounded, and the two lines turned west to meet the main attack. The corporal who had thrown the net over Xara hurriedly scrambled back to his post sliding and slipping on the puddle of Roman blood Xara had left.

The Romans on the west side had blunted the charge of the Catuvellauni women, and they were now jack-stepping forward, using their short swords to methodically hack the surviving women in their path to pieces. The only surprise the Catuvellauni women had left for the Romans was the small children who crawled unseen into the melee to poke up at Roman legs and genitalia with sharpened sticks. Once the soldiers discovered this, spearmen fell to their knees to skewer the small offenders. In the mindless chaos of the battle, they raised their small bodies overhead to the cheers of their comrades.

Behind them, Caratacus main force struck the remainder of the column with all the force he had hoped. The lines of Roman shields and spears, however, blunted the attack. There was a murderous clash of swords and spears, but neither side was able to gain a distinct advantage. The battle would have been a draw if the Catuvellauni blocking force in the middle had held for another few minutes, but they did not. Roman reinforcements from the rear rushed forward minutes after Caratacus had committed his main force. With slashing

Roman's now on both sides, the outcome for the Catuvellauni was no longer in question.

It was a slaughter. Although the Catuvellauni fought like demons, the disciplined Romans beat back each new charge then maneuvered their lines to split the tiring Britons into smaller and smaller groups. Isolated each group, they defeated it with overwhelming numbers as more legionaries became available. It was not a heroic or noble tactic, more like systematic butchery, but the Roman prefect had no intention of giving the Catuvellauni a fair chance; he intended to win.

Within half an hour, most of the tribe's men were dead or wounded; those who were still alive were hardly able to lift their swords. More than nine thousand of the original Catuvellauni force of twelve thousand were dead or so severely wounded that the Romans would finish them off in the field where they had fallen. More than three thousand, including Xara and Caratacus, who had been severely wounded.

The battle at Wolf Glen, a stunning Roman victory, was over by mid-morning.

***

A trumpet sounded in the distance; Metella sheathed his sword and ordered his men to stand easy. A deathly quiet had settled over the valley interrupted only by the sounds of those in pain.

"See to our wounded, Sergeant."

Viper, covered in blood, nodded then issues orders.

"I want the spearmen of the first tent to kill the savages too badly wounded to serve as slaves. Those of

57

the second tent will bind anyone who still lives and can serve as a slave."

Viper nodded again.

"I don't want them roaming; tell them to stay inside our area."

Death squads and capture teams from the cohorts that had not been engaged in the worst of the fighting were already passing through they dead and dying. They were also grouping Catuvellauni who had surrendered or who had less serious wounds into prisoner coffles linked together by chains. Most of them would end their days in a far-off mine or field toiling for the continued glory and enrichment of Rome. Some they would sell to private businesses; most of them would realize the same fate.

Those who were too badly wounded to survive but who could still feel pain, about four-hundred men and fifty women, they tied and herded to a nearby stand of trees. Working systematically, they hoisted them off the ground by their ankles and left them to die. A terrible wailing soon emanated from the trees as blood began to pool in their heads and eyes, creating a terrible mind-splitting pressure. A lucky few died of strokes and seizures in the first few minutes and hours of their hanging. Others died more slowly from exsanguination as wounds bled out and blood vessels ruptured. A small number would survive the entire day in horrible pain and die from exhaustion and dehydration.

This practice of torturing large numbers of enemy combatants was a common practice for the Roman legions. It immediately established the idea in the minds of the prisoners in the slave coffles that they would not tolerate any resistance, and that the price for resistance was extreme pain. It was an effective message.

Xara, dazed and weakened by the blow to her head and securely bound in the straps, watched as a death squad approached her position. She prayed they would kill her quickly, but the corporal who had thrown the net over her quickly put an end to that prayer.

"She killed six of my men," he said to the man in charge of the death squad. "I want her to suffer."

"She's a beauty," the man answered, annoyed, "you would be taking money out of all of our pockets."

"It's my right," he said. "Do I need to call my centurion...?"

The other man, also a corporal, nodded and ordered Xara stripped, manacled, and collared, then he ordered two of his men to deliver her to the Second Legion's chief torturer, their *dux carnifex*. Normally, they would have put her with the coffles of attractive females, now under heavy guard to protect them from the soldier rape. They were too valuable to waste in this way.

"Why do we need to take this one to the *dux carnifex*?" one of her guards asked the other, unaware that Xara spoke Latin.

"The *decanus* has the right to call for her to suffer. He said she killed six of his men."

"This little minx killed six of his men...? Either he's lying or they were pussies."

His friend shrugged. Xara said nothing. If they knew she spoke Latin, they would investigate and find that the Ninth Legion at Rumabo Imperium was looking for her for the killing of their commander. It might not make any difference in the way they tortured her to death, but it might.

"I hear they caught their king, Caratacus," one of the men said. "That's the bastard they should hand over to the torturer, not this little minx."

"I agree. I would like to take her for a spin myself."

Xara fought to keep her expression neutral. The Romans had taken Caratacus...alive!

***

Organizing the surviving Catuvellauni wounded took the Romans the rest of the day. By late afternoon, the legion's columns had reformed and were ready to march. No one wanted to make camp so close to so many corpses, and scouts had already spotted wolves in the distance. Their numbers in this area gave the glen its name. Tonight, they would feast on the dead and the near dead hanging in the trees.

The legate led the way, leading soldiers and chained prisoners slowly past the trees so that everyone could witness the continuing agony of those they had left in the trees. Xara, now a chained prisoner in the torturer's section, could hear their awful wailing echoing in her ears for miles. Caratacus lay chained hand and foot, in a wagon guarded by a century of legionaries. The legate was not taking any chance that he might escape. He would send him to Rome once he recovered for the emperor's judgement and as a reminder of his great victory.

The battle of Wolf's Glen was one of the better days for Rome in Briton.

Chapter Four – Roman Justice

"Begin," the chief torturer, a centurion, ordered.

One of his men pulled on a rope hoisting the first Briton off his feet and suspending him from his wrists. A second man began to whip him with a long lash *ferula,* a slave whip, patiently tearing at his skin until the victim began to scream. They would come back to him later for more. A second man, also naked also with his hands bound was being prepared for hoisting. Three others waited nearby, numb with the prospect of the romans whipping them to death.

They were *exemplars*, examples of Roman justice picked at random from the slave coffles on orders from the legate. He had issued a formal death-by-torture order for all the Catuvellauni prisoners for their rebellion against the empire, but he would only carry out the order on a few. The others they would sell as slaves and the money distributed to the legion's men based on rank.

Centurion Marcus Metella knew the legate's order and the exemplar executions were to cover his ass. If there was a prisoner uprising tonight, he wanted to be able to say he had done all he could to prevent it. In truth, all the legate, Senatorus Plecio, wanted after the bloody battle was a few hours of peace and quiet. He was the third son of a mid-level patrician, and the army was the logical choice of career. He had no particular talent for or interest in the empire's wars of conquest, nor was he convinced that torturing men as a deterrent had the desired effect.

Metella thought he was right; if anything, the screams of those they were torturing exacerbated the risk of a prisoner rebellion, but the army had its ways. They had already demonstrated their serious resolve by the upside-down hanging of the prisoners at Wolf's Glen. Creating a night-long wailing with more painful executions would do nothing to forestall resistance from Brit prisoners who had continued resistance in mind and hinder the much-needed sleep of his men.

They were something, these Brits, he thought as survey the chained prisoners.

He had fought savages in Germania and Gaul, but he had never seen anything like the Britons. Their ferocious savagery was breed into them from birth. The way they hurled themselves at their shield lines had been terrifying; the way they used their women even their children had been inhuman. There was no doubt in Metella's mind that they were half-human and half-animal, perhaps wolf.

Yes, that was probably it, he decided. They probably had the blood of wolves running through their veins. The hideous screams of the second man cut through the night air as his flesh was rent.

Not only was this torture useless in preventing more resistance, but it was also wasteful. The five strong and healthy Britons the torturer was using as exemplars would have brought in good money at the Rumabo auctions, money they needed to keep the men motivated. Their men did not fight for the empire or for the glory of Rome anymore—neither did he—they fought because they were professional soldiers, and professional soldiers needed pay. He was as interested as the next guy in avoiding more bloodshed, but this was just wasteful.

Another hideously long scream of pain cut through the humid night air like a knife. The dense fog settling in over the area muted the light from the hundreds of campfires, and the flickering torches making the scene surreal, like a horrible nightmare that you just could not escape. Maybe this Hellish light will help to keep peace, Metella though turning away from the whipping—the superstitious Brits might think they were really in Hell and...

He began to walk, clasping his hands behind his back as if taking a casual stroll through the ranks of captives and their guards. He wanted his men to see him acting calmly and looking carefree even though he was anything but carefree. Caratacus and his Catuvellaunis were only one of the threats they faced in these northern regions. The Brigantes, the Carveti, the Votadini were all capable of banding together and ambushing the legion. Then, of course, there were the Picts, the fierce northern tribesmen who many believed were cannibals who roasted their captives alive before devouring them. Northern Briton was indeed a savage place.

Another cry of unbearable agony rent the night.

But all this was secondary, he thought. His main concern was not the suffering and death of a few savages, or a potential uprising from the prisoners, or his men's rest, it was the fucking duty the tribune had assigned him and his men. They were not a torture unit, nor were they supposed to guard prisoners. They were a first-class fighting unit, one of the legion's best. Using them for these other purposes was a criminal waste of good fighting men. The tribune should have assigned his unit to the perimeter where they could engage Catuvellauni remnants or raiders. This duty was shit.

He had not openly opposed the order of course, but it was a mistake, a travesty. This was how a fighting unit turned into a rabble; this was how all the fighting discipline he had instilled in his men eroded. This was not fitting work for soldiers, especially men of the second rank.

The second rank...

The legion put its expendable men in the first rank to blunt an enemy charge, and to absorb the worst of the damage. It was the second rank that did most of the fighting. They were the ones who stepped forward to deal with anyone who managed to push his way through the line. Once the first rank had dissipated the energy of an enemy charge, it was his unit and others like it that stepped forward and led the legion's offensive. Who else was going to be the spearhead of an offensive?

It was a sound tactic, one that reflected the Roman qualities of patience, practicality, and process. He had lost count of how many savages they had killed in this way, but the ratio was well over one-hundred enemy to every soldier killed...! But to continue to perform with such deadly effectiveness *he needed good men!* He could not get his...

There was a sudden flurry of movement from the second man, and he turned to watch him kick his legs out wildly as if trying to climb invisible stairs. It was unnerving to watch brave men die like this with so little dignity, even Brit savages, but much of what the legion did was without dignity. Executing prisoners, killing the wounded after a battle, interrogations, reprisals were all good examples. These were not appropriate duty for a fighting unit. They wore away at a man's self-image, his humanity, his fighting spirit, and most importantly his discipline. This last was especially dangerous.

He had wanted to explain this to the tribune, but there had not been any opportunity. The last thing he wanted his men to see was him arguing with a superior officer over the appropriateness of an order. Letting the men know that he had issues would just add to their disquiet.

He stepped carefully around a *medici* (doctor) operating on wounded prisoner. It was good business to save as many as they could; just as it was nonsense to kill them for no good reasons. Other wounded prisoners were sitting on the ground waiting. Blood and dirt still covered their bodies in addition to the blue woad they used as warpaint. They were stoically bearing their pain as they listened to the man suffering under the whip. Some commanders thought that having legionaries witness the torture of the enemy was a morale builder, just as important as the distribution of profits from the slave sales.

In his opinion, they were wrong. Professional soldiers did not or should not get so personally involved that they welcomed their enemy's pain. He had never understood the purpose of torturing the enemy to intimidate them. For each one they intimidated, there were ten who were they incentivized to fight even harder.

I have nothing against these Brits myself, he thought. They are simply fighting for their land and their freedom, just like any animal would. They have no idea of the benefits of civilization that comes with Roman conquest. It's unfortunate that they are so ignorant, so savage as to oppose the advantages that Rome's offers, but it was also understandable

Another medic was busy sewing a soldier's sliced arm back together. The man, really a boy, looked up and muttered, "*Vires et Decus,*" proudly through gritted teeth.

"Strength and Honor," Marcus replied, repeating the legion's motto back to him, but there was little pride in his voice. This torture did not represent strength and honor; this was more a display of weakness and dishonor.

This victory over the Catuvellauni wasn't very honorable in his mind. Killing hundreds of wounded prisoners, waving speared children overhead like battle flags; these were the acts of savages not Roman soldiers. Our savagery undermines our mission to civilize these people, he thought. It was also dangerous for discipline. During the battle, when the men had waved the speared children overhead, they had spurred a killing spree, an undisciplined rampage. That was the only time during the battle he had been afraid. The Britons could not defeat the machine that was the Roman legion, but they could defeat an unruly mob of Roman scum.

He walked past a group of perhaps male prisoners chained to tree trunks they had left standing inside the stockade. They were watching the flogging with a burning hatred in their eyes. We are inciting them to violence with this torture. It is exactly the wrong tactic. "Strength and honor" should not just be something wounded soldiers say to sound brave; it should be the creed we live by in this savage place.

There should have been more prisoners, he thought. We should have allowed the prisoners to help their wounded comrades. Many of those the death squads killed were salvageable—there would have been scores more slaves for the block—but everyone's blood had been running hot including the legate's. He should have been the coolest of us.

A large group of women sat chained behind the men. They would also have a place in the slave wagons. A third, smaller group of moderately attractive women sat just beyond. The legion's slave handlers had earmarked them for the legion's use. They would serve in the barracks...and probably die there.

He walked on. A small group of maybe forty or fifty women sat chained in the corner of the fort's wall. Marcus knew from the heavy guard that they were the women destined for the auction block and for sexual service. Their guards were alert; there had already been a few incidents of rape. Wealthy Romans would buy some of these women as household servants. It was prestigious to have attractive female slaves around the house. The best-looking ones from this bunch would go to the brothel owners. There are some real beauties here, he noticed. They will fetch us a good price even though Britons typically did not make good servants or good whores.

"Too much animal, not enough human in them," an experienced slaver had told him once in Rumabo. "Even after they are hard-trained, you never know when they will revert to the wild. I've heard stories of men losing their cocks to Brit women whom they have disciplined for years. If you want my advice, Centurion," the man had warned him, "don't ever put your cock in a Brit mouth without protection. Always use a ring gag or wooden jaw blockers. Of course, you lose a lot of the pleasure of mouth-fucking when they can't close the lips around your cock or create a proper suction. A girl's soft mouth is supposed to feel like a cunt—but the alternative is too terrible to contemplate."

He had been right, Metella decided. Britons were too animal-like to engage in such human behavior as fellatio. Advertising that a Brit was a good cocksucker was deceptive and dangerous. There should be a law if some kind to prevent slavers from mixing Brits in with humans.

This was why compliant and curvaceous Hispanics were fetching the highest block prices these days in Rome with Gallic women close behind. Still, some buyers probably thought that a lean Brit might be exciting to own for a while. The problem with that kind of thinking was that a slave could devolve into an expensive plaything fit only for punishment.

The whip cut through the air again followed by another hideous scream. It was a high-pitched screech, the sound a woman would make. We're not just torturing them, he thought, we're taking away their pride, turning fierce warriors into screaming women. This virtual castration will also incite them to violence. No man, even one destined for slavery, wanted to become a woman. This lot had been warriors, now they were slaves, we didn't need to make them into women.

Another painful outcry…

Maybe the commander is right. Maybe this is a fitting end for this lot. The Catuvellauni deserved eternal punishment for sacrificing their children as they had done. If anyone needed any further proof that they were animals in human form, this was it. We invited them to join the civilized world, to participate in Roman progress, and they spit in our faces then send their children at us for us to slaughter. Cooperation with Rome would not be easy for them, but it would elevate them from the mud of their sub-human existence. Instead, they choose to fight.

If the Catuvellauni had chosen friendship, they would all still be alive. They deserved…

He caught the sudden flash of movement and moved just in time to avoid having his leg broken. The girl had launched herself at him like a snake, striking at his knee with the heel of her bare foot. Even with his evasive maneuver, her blow was substantial, and he staggered back and fell heavily on his rump looking foolish. I am Rome's representative, he though, and now Rome looks foolish. As if to confirm, the Brit slaves nearby stirred, and smiles appeared on several faces.

Had he not moved, the blow would have broken his leg, but after years of battle Metella knew how to absorb a hit. Still, the pain was so severe that it left him momentarily stunned. The girl stared at him defiantly, smiling in triumph. Her collar chain was still vibrating from the force of her vicious lunge. The sergeant in charge of the guard detail rushed over to help him to his feet.

"Please stay away from that one, Centurion," Viper said quietly. "She's wild...bit one of my men so badly we had to take him to the *medici*. She's for the rack as soon as the chief torturer has time. The word is that she killed six of our men on the western side of the column. I should have staked her to the ground while we waited for the torturer...sorry. I just have not had time with all screaming of the exemplars. It's stirring up the animals something awful."

He pointed back with his chin towards the man twisting in his bondage.

Metella turned towards the man still a little dazed. Sergeant Spurius Vipsanius was the unit's unofficial disciplinarian. The men called him Viper.

A fitting name, Metella thought. Sergeant Vipsanius's reputation for cruelty was well-known. He was a good fighter though, which was why Metella tolerated him in his unit. It was also good to have a man

69

like Viper around when they pulled this kind of wrongful duty. Getting prisoners to obey under normal conditions was hard enough, but with the sound of torture in the air, it was next to impossible.

Metella got clumsily to his feet and knelt, kneading his bruised leg then turned towards the girl who had struck him. She was naked with a long smooth female body that had a compelling strength to it. Her hardness will turn off many slave buyers, he decided. She's too lean, too sinewy. Still, she was a beauty; she would make every cock in the room hard when she stood on the block. But she wasn't destined for the block, he remembered. Viper had said she was destined for the torturer's rack.

Waste...!

"Six men, sergeant...!" he said skeptically, getting to his feet. This little wisp of a girl defeated six Roman legionaries in combat...? I find that very hard to believe. It sounds like one of those stories soldier like to tell each other."

In truth, he was thinking it might be true. The look in her eyes was pure rage, the kind of rage that could propel a savage to do incredible things.

But to forego the profits from her sale...because she had fought hard and well...? This seemed especially wasteful to him. Even with such a savage temperament, sleek long-legged beauties like her sold well, mostly to sadists—those who enjoy taming slaves just to watch them suffer. Such men were always lurking around the slave auctions, always on the lookout for inexpensive beauties too wild for anyone to tame let alone civilize. Many of them were just agents for rich Romans, men and women who worshipped pain.

The torturer's whip struck again sending another hideous scream into the night air.

Maybe she has gone mad, Metella wondered. A battle can do that. It can push someone over the edge, make them oblivious to consequences.

He stepped forward and roughly grabbed the girl's long hair pulling her head back hard. She tried to resist, but the guards had widely manacled her wrists and locked them onto a waist chain. She just stared defiantly waiting for him to kill her. No, she wasn't mad, he decided. Years on the battlefield had taught him to tell the difference between madness and rage. He felt a moment of relief. No one, not even the sadists, would pay anything for an insane Brit bitch. Most slavers destroyed mad slaves without a second thought. They were not even worth torturing.

Metella felt his cock getting harder; spirited women excited him. Like with wild horses and dogs, taming a woman with such courage was an interesting diversion. This hellion probably did kill several legionaries during the battle. I wonder how she survived, he asked himself, then answered his own question as his knuckles felt the bumps on the back of her head. Someone had clubbed her into unconsciousness probably after he had netted her.

He dropped her head and calmly stood over her for several seconds. She looked up, the triumph in her face was gone. She had expected him to fly into a rage, to strike back at her, to lose control. She had anticipated that her kick would anger him enough to put on a show, something she might be able to use to further ridicule him, something that would underscore her courage and diminish his...only this centurion wasn't cooperating.

The rack...

71

The rack was too good for her. She deserved the humiliation of...of a barrack's whore, Metella thought, as a wave of pain boiled up from his knee. The men typically tied a barrack's whore by her wrists and ankles to a rope bedframe then hooded and raped her as long as she could survive. They took precautions against cock biting by knocking out her teeth. It was a painful few days for the slave, usually terminated by a merciful legionary running a knife across her throat.

Too ignoble a death for one so brave, he decided suddenly. She was a fighter; she deserved a more fitting end than racking or barracks whore. She saw the expression on his face and tried to spit at him, but her insolent smile was gone.

Your insolence will get her killed in the barracks, he thought. The men won't tolerate it, they have lost too many friends today. They will torture a whore who resists; if they can't fuck her, they will get their satisfaction by hurting her. It starts with someone poking her with a stick and evolves into real torture as they become fascinated with her suffering. He had seen it happen before. This vicious war against the Brits had become very dirty and very personal.

He studied her more closely. She was young, perhaps eighteen, and clearly trained as a fighter. The lean muscles in her arms could only come from long hours wielding a sword of a knife. But there was no mistaking her sex. Her hard pointed breasts tipped by a pair of sharply protruding nipples struck out proudly, counterbalanced by her high round ass. His eyes moved to her pubic mound which she did nothing to hide, it was swollen nearly as large as a man's balls. He could feel his

72

prick straining. It would be interesting to fuck this one, he thought, interesting and exciting.

But she was destined for the rack…

He stepped down hard on her neck chain. The sudden action slammed the side of her face into the hard ground. She squirmed and her body undulated like a speared snake, but she had no leverage without the use of her arms. The other slaves watching pushed themselves back as far as the coffle chain would allow.

"Bring me a slave whip," he growled to Viper.

"Shit," Viper muttered under his breath then angrily snapped his head at one of his men, who ran to fetch the leather.

It was clear that Viper disapproved of the centurion's interference but was afraid to object openly. Centurion Marcus Metella was a hard ass, with a fierce temper, and a reputation for dealing violently with insubordination. Arguing with him was ill-advised, especially in a matter of personal honor.

The centurion should have just walked away and let him deal with her, Viper thought. He would have staked her to the ground as a troublemaker. The girl was already destined to suffer on the rack. What more could Metella do to her?

"Let me punish the bitch for you, Centurion," Viper offered persuasively. "Come back in an hour. I assure you that she will beg to lick your balls."

Viper's tone was respectful but surprisingly insistent; he had a job to do, and the centurion was making that job harder. Metella stared at him then extended his arm for the whip. The soldier who had fetched the implement stepped forward quickly to hand it to him.

"Her legs…," he said, still staring into Viper's eyes.

73

"You two…on her legs," Viper ordered sullenly.

Two of his men jumped to comply, grabbing the girl's kicking feet.

"This animal struck me with her foot," the centurion announced to no one in particular.

"The rack is too lenient for her. I want her impaled."

Xara raised her head and looked up at him as if she had understood his words. The other men in Viper's charge smiled, the impalement of a beautiful woman would be an interesting diversion from the hard work of guarding prisoners. Viper had a different idea and pointed to the side to speak to him privately. The centurion followed.

"Impaled, Centurion…? You want this animal impaled for kicking out at you? We don't have the equipment or the time to impale a savage right now. Impalement takes a lot of work especially if we need to calm down the other slaves at the same time. They get riled up when we kill a young woman.

"More riled than fogging five of their number as examples, Sergeant?" Marcus interrupted.

Viper didn't rise to the bait.

"The floggings were the tribune's idea…

"Let her go to the barracks, Sir, if you think that the rack is now too good for her. Believe me, the men will make her pay for her insult to you a thousand times over, and you won't have to be bothered punishing her yourself."

"Stand at attention, Sergeant," Marcus ordered quietly.

Viper knew that tone and immediately snapped to attention. He knew he'd gone too far…

74

"Sergeant Spurius Vipsanius, more commonly known among the men as Viper," Metella spit out disdainfully, reminding him of their respective ranks.

It was common for centurions to be publicly contemptuous of the sadists in their ranks. Viper didn't like it, but he was used to it.

"Are you questioning my order, Sergeant?"

"No, Centurion, I'm not," Viper answered nervously. "It's just that I was told to hold this whore for the rack and to have the other prisoners tied down for the night before we dose the campfires. The time and the men required to impale this bitch will make it impossible for me to comply with my prior order. Which order should I follow, Centurion?"

Another cry of pain was loud and strong. The guards had hoisted a new Brit off the ground for his whipping. Marcus glanced up again the long scream tore through the night air. Viper was right; the public torture of the girl on top of the floggings would stir up the slaves and cause trouble. He nodded; Viper was dealing with a legitimate conflict of orders.

"Then, Sergeant, we will need to deal with the exact method of her termination in another way. For now, I will have to be satisfied with a whipping. We can't have the other prisoners thinking that we will tolerate such an assault...can we?"

Viper shrugged. The Centurion turned back to the girl.

"Turn her over," he ordered.

The two men corkscrewed her long legs, forcefully her to rotate onto her stomach. Her manacled hands were now trapped underneath her body.

"Spread her legs."

The men pulled her legs as far apart as they could go, exposing her asshole and cunt to the night air. A third man, unbidden, lifted her by her waist chain and pushed a log under her waist. Her ass was now high in the air. Marcus paused to admire her firm thighs and legs. The position was highlighting her calves and hamstring muscles and forcing her legs open had dimpled her ass cheeks. She twisted her head to stare up at him, still defiant but now clearly scared. Another scream from the whipping her of how much pain a whip could cause.

Metella smiled at her again then struck several light blows with the *ferula* between her ass cheeks. She twisted with the sharp cutting pain but remained silent. Suddenly, he snapped the whip in her ass crack with force. The girl's body jerked upward, and she screamed, momentarily drowning out the cries from the whipping. The *ferula* was designed for maximum pain, especially when applied to such tender body parts, but it would not kill, nor would it leave permanent scars. It was a perfect choice for a trophy slave.

Xara recovered quickly and her head snapped back to snarl at the centurion. He struck her again then again, a dozen times in all. Her body was twitching uncontrollably when he stopped.

"You see how savage this one is, Sergeant," Metella said, as if the whipping had proven his point. "She hasn't once begged for mercy...much too evil for the cross and too wild for the barracks...a danger to the men. You should have seen this yourself."

He tossed the whip contemptuously to the ground at Viper's feet.

"No, she's not safe to be a barrack's whore. She's only fit to die as an example to the others."

76

He paused for a moment, thinking.

"But I do understand your dilemma, Sergeant," he added slowly. "Impalement will take time and the men have other work to do tonight."

He paused again as if trying to think of another option.

"Very well, deliver her to my tent tonight after you have secured the others. I will see to her punishment myself. We can show her body to the others in the morning."

Viper started to object then was suddenly quiet. Men, even officers, were not permitted to take slaves from the slave pool for their personal use, especially one of the condemned. It affected morale. The very-correct Marcus Metella was about to break one of the legion's strictest rules.

This could work to his advantage, Viper thought. Not only that, why should he argue this point with an officer? Being right in these matters counted for nothing; discipline was the first concern in the legion. If the centurion wanted to break regulations to fuck a beautiful slave, then let other more senior officers deal with him. This wasn't his fight.

"Yes Sir. I'll have her cleaned up and delivered to you as soon as I've finished with the prisoners." There was a hint of conspiracy in his voice.

Officers! Viper thought, they were all assholes. This might work out well for me though. Marcus Metella was well-regarded and the protégé of Prefect Gaius Lepidi. He was also a favorite of the legate. Having such a man in his debt could only help his fortunes. Besides, he had already come to the same conclusion about the girl—she was worthless to them, too savage to sell as a slave and perhaps, as the centurion had said, even too guilty for the rack. What difference did it make if she died at Metella's hand servicing his cock?

"...As ordered," Viper added for the benefit of those legionaries listening to their exchange; he finished smartly sweeping his arm across his chest in salute. There would be no question later about who had ordered what.

Metella stared at him searching for any sign of disrespect. Sergeants often felt that they commanded the legion rather than the officers. Even a sadist like Viper thinks he knows better, Metella thought. He turned quickly and left without another word.

Xara watched the centurion walk away. Tears of pain were streaming down her face. Her ass and legs felt as if they were on fire. Suddenly, she had the bitter thought that maybe she had picked the wrong Roman to humiliate.

Chapter Five - The *Arcus-Atrox*

As promised, Viper delivered the slave Xara to Metella's tent later that evening.

"The slave...as you ordered, Centurion," Viper announced, saluting formally in the tent's doorway.

The girl was still naked, but Viper had had her cleaned. He had also had her strapped her to an *arcus-atrox*.

The *arcus-atrox*, which literally meant "cruel bow," was a common instrument of torture in the legions. It was an iron longbow in which the victim, bound by her arms and legs to the metal served as a human bow string. A small crank at the foot of the iron facilitated the bending of the metal and adjusting its tension. The torturer could use the two handles on the iron to carry it and use the iron ring at the top of the shaft to suspend it and its hapless victim.

Depending on the tension, the device could cause excruciating pain at the joints or even pull limbs from their sockets with a slow, steady pressure. Torturers used it sometimes for flogging in the field when no trees were available, and the whip-master wanted the victim's skin and body painfully taut.

Metella stared angrily at Viper then stood aside so that two strong soldiers could carry the straining Xara into his tent. They stood her upright, suspending the arcus-atrox from the main tent pole with a heavy chain. Xara tried to maintain a neutral expression, but it was impossible with the pain, even though Viper had set the bow's tension to moderate tautness, one appropriate for whipping.

79

"I have set the tension for whipping," he confirmed. "I assumed you would want to start her off with a whipping. You do know how to operate the *arcus-atrox*, Centurion...?"

Marcus didn't answer, he just glared at him for several seconds trying to detect any sign of disrespect in his voice.

"Why did you put her in this device, Sergeant?" he asked. "I didn't order it."

"You said you wanted her impaled, Centurion," Viper answered respectfully. "I just assumed you wanted her to suffer maximum pain until that happened. When used properly, the *arcus-atrox* can produce the same amount of pain as impalement, Sir, I assure you. She will certainly pay for her offense to you in this."

Viper knelt and put his hand on the bow's crank.

"Just wind this another few notches and her muscles will begin to tear or use the slave whip. Her writhing under the *ferula* will also tear muscles. There was smirk on his face, a look that said, *I know you want to fuck her*. Marcus remained still, staring at him with steely eyes until the smirk disappeared.

"Since you wanted to punish her yourself," Viper rushed to explain, "I just assumed you would want to use an *arcus-atrox*." When Marcus still didn't reply, he added nervously. "It's the easiest method of torture when you are working...alone."

Marcus eyes narrowed to slits. Viper's emphasis of the word "alone" was a clear message that he knew what Metella wanted from the girl.

"I, ah, I just assumed...," he added lamely, now completely flummoxed by the glare.

80

It was not unheard of for a centurion to summarily execute an insubordinate soldier.

Metella considered his options. The sergeant's obvious disrespect demanded a response of some kind. He could have him disciplined, but the Prefect, Gaius Lepidi, was a stickler for correct behavior between the officers and the men. He would need more than a suspicion to charge this worm with insubordination, he would need tangible evidence and witnesses. That was the problem; he doubted that any of the sergeant's men would turn on him for a centurion.

There was also another aspect of the man's behavior to consider. Viper was showing a remarkable degree of initiative in this matter. Most of the peasant-soldiers in the legion couldn't even speak when confronted by an officer, let alone act intelligently. Most of them didn't have the intellectual capacity for the subtle defiance the sergeant had displayed. In a strange way, delivering the girl himself and putting her in the *arcus-atrox* showed the man's value.

Marcus knelt by the crank and considered winding it, dislocating the girl's limbs. This would remove any doubt that his intentions were "honorable." Instead, he turned towards the sergeant and whispered.

"I will personally flay you alive with a sharp knife, Viper, if any report of this reaches the prefect," Marcus whispered menacingly. "Do you understand me, viper?"

Viper looked at him and nodded; this centurion didn't make idle threats. The rumor was that Marcus Metella would be the next *primus pilus*, centurion of the first cohort, senior centurion of the entire legion. Defying him in a matter of personal honor was a foolish risk. Metella's threat of flaying him alive, of cutting off all his skin, was not just talk…he could do it; he would do it.

"We lose prisoners all the time, Centurion, for many reasons," he answered quietly, too softly for the guards outside to hear. "I have already replaced this bitch with another from the slave pool. She is the one I will deliver to the chief torturer for racking. Your girl is no longer part of our accounting; in effect, she doesn't exist any longer. You are free to do with her as you see fit, to use her in any way you like. If she should happen to die under your…your justified interrogation, just send for me. I will have her body dumped quietly into one of the latrine pits. No one will find her there."

Marcus thought about what the man had said then glanced at the girl suspended in the arcus-atrox. There was understanding in her eyes, that she quickly tried to hide it from him. Could she be listening? That was impossible; Brit savages didn't speak Latin. She could not possibly understand what they were saying. She was just inferring some meaning from the tone of their voices. He turned back to Viper.

He didn't like partnering with a slimy character like him, but it was necessary for the moment. He wanted the girl and there was no other way. Viper lowered his voice and spoke again with disgusting intimacy.

"This is a better end for her anyway, Centurion. I don't like to see the pretty ones racked or disfigured in the barracks. It's an awful waste…very un-Roman. It's better that she finish her time beautiful and intact, cursing our names in honorable torture at your capable hands."

The thought of the girl's upcoming torture reminded him of something. He reached into his sack and produced a leather ring gag.

"Please...use this on her during the worst of it, Centurion. We wouldn't want her screams to draw too much attention, nor would we want her to injure you during..." He smiled knowingly. "After all this 'discipline' is unauthorized and..."

"Unauthorized?" Marcus growled in a low voice. "The only authority you need, Sergeant, is my order. Do you understand?"

Viper smiled and nodded his head.

"Of course, Centurion, of course, I did not mean...I was just..."

Marcus held up one hand for silence and reached into his belt with the other. It was the tradition in the legion for officers to reward the personal service of ordinary soldiers with a few coins. Viper smiled then saluted once again. By accepting the offering, he was sealing the deal between them. They would both forget the centurion's regulatory offense in taking a prisoner and Viper's impertinence. The sergeant saluted again, bowed obsequiously, and left closing the tent flap behind him.

***

Marcus stood still for a few seconds considering what he'd done. Following the dictates of one's cock was not a very smart career move, he thought. Everything he'd done this evening since the girl had kicked him was against regulations. Officers didn't take prisoners for personal punishment or for sexual purposes. He could easily lose his promised promotion to centurion of the first cohort; they could even demote or discipline him. The legion was his life; why was he risking his life for a piece of Brit ass? If he wanted sex, there were officially sanctioned ways to get it…this was not one of them.

He stepped close to the girl's lean body; the *arcus-atrox* was turning slowly around the tent pole. The muscles in her arms were straining against the bow's inhuman strength. He put his hand on her bare hip to stop the motion, and she stared at him with the same hate-filled eyes he'd seen earlier. She was clearly scared, terrified, but the fear was not paralyzing her, it was exciting her. There was even a hint of curiosity in her eyes.

Curiosity…?

This surprised him. Even the most hardened fighter was afraid of Roman torture. It was a reasonable fear. The legions had made a science out of inflicting pain, and she had already guessed what was coming. He could see the understanding in her eyes.

"You *should* be afraid of me, girl, very afraid," he said aloud to himself knowing she couldn't understand. "With this terrible device and a little patience, I can make you suffer in ways that you can't even imagine."

She continued to stare at him. It was clear that she hated and despised him. There was no hint of respect or even grudging acknowledgement that he was the victor in their personal battle, or that he was now the master of her fate.

He inserted the crank into its hole and tightened the bow by one notch. Her taut body vibrated with the increased tension; he had stretched her to her limit. He could see the leather at her biceps and thighs digging into her skin; he could see her veins pulsating in her underarms; he watched her hands and feet fluttering, trying to resist the metal's pull. Her eyes remained locked on his, filled with terrible pain but still defiant.

He turned the crank another notch then stopped; she had closed her eyes and started panting. Her muscles must be screaming now, her joints on the verge of tearing. After a moment she opened her eyes and resumed her contemptuous staring.

"You're not afraid yet, because you don't really understand what the tearing pain is going to be like. I can literally pull your arms and legs from their sockets with this thing then fuck you as you writhe helplessly on the floor." He was speaking his evil thoughts aloud, trying to scare her with his tone.

He ran his hand down her long torso again, lingering over her hard nipple. He could feel himself hardening and reached down inside his pants to play with himself as he stroked her trembling body. His excitement was growing as she continued to resist the tearing.

Suddenly, she shuddered, in a way that he could not interpret as anything but a sexual response. It was the movement of a young woman yearning for sexual penetration. For the first time he saw emotions other than hatred and rage in her eyes. She was...embarrassed, her body had betrayed her...and it wasn't finished embarrassing her.

He quickly released the tension a notch and resumed his petting. The more he touched her, the more pronounced her sexual response. He felt her shudder again then steel herself against more involuntary reactions. She was still fighting her out-of-control emotions when she climaxed. The act was unmistakable in its content and a complete surprise to Metella in its violence. There was a final involuntary shudder, a last contraction, and it was over.

They looked at each other, both astonished. Her body had rebelled against her mind, responding to a powerful sexual need that she was unable to control. He smiled. In a strange way—they now shared an intimate secret.

"So, there's more to you than rage, eh," he whispered softly. "Let me see what else you are hiding from me."

He picked up the slave whip and struck her hard on the underarm. Her arms were folded behind her head and her wrists tied to the cord at her neck so the stoke showed up first as choking then a red welt began to form; beyond this, she didn't react. He struck again slightly lower with the same response...lower...the same...lower. He started again from the top. On the tenth blow she cried out and there was a flicker of fear in her eyes. He struck several more time in the same spot. She tried desperately to hold back her cries, but she could not. She screamed then looked at him with renewed hatred, not for the pain he was causing but for forcing her to scream. It was an ignominious response for a warrior. He laid another series of blows across the same spot on the other underarm until she was twisting in agony then he grabbed her Venus mound and stuck a finger inside her cunt. She was soaking wet, and her vaginal muscles were trembling. She shuddered and climaxed again even more violently than the first time.

He stood back and laughed. She had an incredibly strong sexual response even to pain.

Her eyes were just coming down and her mouth was open, sucking in air. Slowly she calmed then finally stopped twitching. She stared at him with a loathing so deep that it seemed to create a cloud of hate between them. He stared back, waiting for her to break eye contact, waiting for her to beg him for a quick death in her savage Briton tongue.

"*Ignavus* (coward)," she hissed in Latin through clenched teeth.

He blinked, thinking he had just imagined what he'd heard, then he struck her several times under her exposed breast. She stared at him until the pain was too much to bear then she screamed. He paused until her screaming had subsided then massaged her mound until she came again. After, he began again. It took him five iterations of whipping and stimulation before she was trembling and softly wailing with the sexual terror he wanted. Again, he waited until her writhing stopped. She had the same look of loathing on her face.

"*Ignavus* (coward)," she whispered again, painfully but with even more disdain.

Marcus stopped and stepped back, shocked. There was no question now—he had not misheard.

"You speak Latin?" he asked incredulously.

No answer, only the same hateful stare.

He considered what she'd said. There were rumors that the Britons were torturing Roman prisoners, forcing them to teach them Latin. Perhaps she had learned the word from some poor soldier that she had skinned alive or burned to death. He turned her body in the bow and laid a series of violent cane blows on her tight ass then waited again while she recovered. Her recovery from his pain was now taking noticeably longer. She would be screaming at each blow in an hour or two. That's when she would need a gag Viper had given him. The chief torturer wasn't the only expert at torture in the legion.

"*Ignavus* (coward)," she hissed again, her bare, curved back mocking him.

"Is that the only word you know," he asked, curious. "How did you learn it? Was it from a Roman prisoner? Did you burn him, peel off his skin? Tell me!"

He turned her again so that she was facing him. She glared defiantly then unbelievably spit out her answer in flawless Latin.

"No, *Ignavus*, I wouldn't touch any of you monsters even to bring you pain. I learned your filthy language as a prisoner from other Roman pigs like you."

Marcus stepped back, astonished. Her Latin was perfect; it was as if she'd been speaking it for years. The legions had taken thousands of Briton prisoners. Could she be telling the truth? Could she have learned their language in Roman captivity...well enough to converse? Had she escaped?"

"And yes, you were right earlier, *Ignavus*," she continued, quickly recovering her breath. "I would have killed the men in your barracks if I could. You did the right thing taking me off the chain to personally torture me. That's what I would have done to you for challenging my honor. I would have you licking my ass clean and screaming like a woman before the night was over if you were in my hands."

He stepped back astonished. There were only a handful of savages in all of Briton that could speak Latin this well and most of them had were working for the army in Rome. As far as he knew, their legions had no one who had truly mastered the two languages. She was a major find of significant military importance.

He got to his knee and cranked the device slowly reducing the tension. The girl shuddered involuntarily as the awful pull lessened.

"I am Marcus Metella, soon to be senior centurion of the 1st Centuria, 1st Cohort, Second Legion," he said quietly. "I am not a coward and will not be called one especially by a cunt, by a Brit slave."

He reached back for his short sword and held the point against her exposed throat.

"You will not refer to me as coward again. She looked up at him smiled, unafraid."

"Yes, *Ignavus*," she said slowly with an unblinking stare. "I hear you, *Ignavus*, but I choose not to obey." She was taunting him, manipulating him into killing her.

He removed the sword from her throat and untied the ropes holding her in the *arcus-atrox*. She dropped to the floor and curled into a ball as her muscles and joints howled in sudden pain. He sat down cross-legged and laid the sword down on the floor between them. Slowly, she recovered then rose warily to her knees facing him, spreading her legs immodestly wide in a fighting stance. She would not be easily bound again in the *arcus-atrox*.

"Releasing me was a very dangerous thing to do, *Ignavus*. Your foolish pride might cost you more than you think, perhaps even your life."

"I doubt it," he answered coolly, watching her eyes.

Marcus Metella had joined the legion at fourteen, fought in a hundred battles, and killed more men than he could count. He had little fear of the naked girl across from him. She was right though, there was risk, but somehow, he knew that a demonstration of his courage and strength was the only way to reach her poisoned mind.

She leaned back on her haunches still rubbing her thin arms. He would not cow her by his demeanor or rush her into making her move before she was ready. He waited patiently, continuing to stare into her eyes. When her attack came it was blindingly quick and violent.

Instead of reaching for the sword as he had expected, she slashed at his eyes, catching and ripping an eyelid with her fingernail. Blood poured out blinding him on one side. In an instant, she capitalized on her advantage by leaping to his blind side while reaching for the hilt of the sword. She was incredibly fast, so fast it was hard for him to follow.

Metella ignored the cut and the blood. He had years of personal combat experience and knew instinctively that the only real danger to him lay with the sword. She could hurt him in other ways of course, but the only way for her to wound him mortally was with the sword. Consequently, he was ready when she moved to retrieve it.

His muscled arm swept around, and his fist caught her on the side of the head. She fell, dazed, to the ground, and he was on her in an instant, pulling first one than the other wrist into the small of her back. She began to twist with the strength of a wild animal, but it was too late. His weight was too much for her to dislodge and he was also strong, stronger than she ever imagined.

"Never go for the weapon, girl, until your opponent is helpless," he whispered, cruelly pulling her bound arms up painfully high on her back with one hand. "I would have tried for the other eye if I were you. You would have had a real chance if I had blood in both eyes. You have the speed and the strength; this tent is on the perimeter of the camp; you might have made it over the stockade to freedom if you had not gone for the kill too soon."

She struggled to break free, but his hand was like a vise. He was right; she had tried to kill him too soon. Why...? She was a better fighter than that.

He grabbed the leather thongs from his sandals and quickly used them to bind each of her wrists to their opposite elbow. Her arms made a perfect square behind her back. He pushed his knee between her flailing legs forcing them open then fiercely pulled off his tunic exposing his cock.

"I ordered you impaled for striking me this evening. Now I will carry out that sentence."

He pushed his cock inside her with the force of a bull fucking a cow. She screamed and tried to squeeze her cunt closed, but his legs were too strong, and she was too wet. The only thing her violent struggling did was to excite the muscles in her vulva and caused it to spasm which nearly brought the centurion to ejaculate prematurely.

"This isn't going to be over so quickly," he whispered into her ear, suppressing his climax, and pushing himself further inside...to the hilt. Xara twisted and screamed in frustration causing her cunt to continue to squeeze his cock in sudden hard bursts. In seconds, they were moving together in a fierce dance that was half copulation and half mortal combat. They came together in an explosion that left them both stunned and breathless. Marcus lay on her with his full weight, exhausted. She could only breathe in short, stunted gasps.

He recovered first and slid back along her body, grabbing her ankles. Savagely, he bent her legs back and tied them to her bent arms in a painful hogtie. She was still and quiet as if stunned by the events of the last few minutes. Marcus lay down on the floor beside her, his face inches from hers then he pushed her disheveled hair out of her face.

"Do you use your real sword now, Centurion, and slit my throat?" she whispered.

No answer

"...Or perhaps continue with my torture like a good Roman?"

"Neither...," he answered after a while.

It was obvious from his tone that he had no regard for her pain.

"I need to rest then I'll probably fuck you again. Maybe use my ring gag so I can fuck you in the mouth. We'll get back to your torture at some point. There's plenty of time for that."

She turned her head away from him and closed her eyes, unwilling to let him to see her expression. She was a warrior and warriors didn't allow their captors to fuck them...and they didn't suck cock. But she didn't know how to prevent either of those things. This Roman was going to get whatever he wanted from her no matter what she did to prevent it.

Hidden deep in her mind, however, she knew that the Roman was not the problem. She was. Her body had committed treason against her mind, and she knew that there was no escape from its continuing betrayal. For the first time since her escape from the Roman camp at Rumabo, she was truly afraid...of her own feelings.

Chapter Six - The Plan

Three Roman legionaries had run from the battle at Wolf Glen. It was not a lot out of five thousand men, and given the ferocity of the fighting, but the officers considered any number of deserters too many. They needed to remind the men that the very worst crime a legionary could commit was to leave their comrades in battle and run.

The three stood naked with their hands tied behind facing the assembled legion, everyone except the guards assigned to the prisoners was watching. Prefect Gaius Lepidi, the legates advisor on military tactics and procedure, stood on the rough platform in the cold morning air looking out over the troops standing in perfect formation. It was his job to address them during before the legion's torturer administered the deserters' punishment.

"These men ran during the battle," he began in a deep resounding voice that echoed through the ranks like the low rumble of thunder. "They ran," he repeated, "…and they have admitted their guilt." He paused dramatically for several long seconds. "They have dishonored themselves and the Second Legion." He paused again to add emphasis to his next statement. "They put all of our lives at risk by their selfish and cowardly actions."

Despite his humble roots, Gaius Lepidi was a master of oration. It was a skill he had acquired in thirty-five years of addressing soldiers. Instinctively, he knew that this was the moment for a more intimate message, and he moderated his voice from its senatorial grandeur to a man-to-man intimacy.

"Bothers!" The word was a plea. "We survive in this savage land because we can count on each other, no matter what. We are victorious because of our commitment to stand together, no matter what we face. All sane men are afraid in a battle, but we overcome those fears out of loyalty to our comrades. Yes, we swear allegiance to Rome, to the legion, but it is our love for one another that keeps us alive."

The prefect's speech was affecting even the accused cowards, who were hanging their heads in shame, unable to meet the unrelenting stares of the men in the ranks.

"Anyone who would leave his comrade to die in the middle of a battle simply because he is afraid is…a true coward and we cannot tolerate cowards in our ranks."

Lepidi had given this same speech hundreds of times before, and each time it moved the men, each time was like the first. If he had ordered it, they would have torn the offenders apart limb from limb.

"These cowards deserve the worst punishment we can imagine, but they were once our friends. We represent civilization in this wild land and the savages watch the way we treat each other. I therefore absolve them of the punishment they well deserve and banish these cowards from our ranks and from the protection of our walls."

He turned slowly to the sergeant in charge of the guard and nodded his head. The man unsheathed his sword and moved behind the first man to cut his bonds. He did the same for the others. A drum started and he ordered the three to turn and march. The drama continued as they walked forward to the drum's slow beat, their genitals swinging between their legs. The heads of the men in the ranks turned away as they passed in front of each of men. Slowly, they left through the gate, and it closed behind them with a final thud.

The prefect nodded again, and the sergeant of the guard yelled, "Dismissed!"

The sentence of banishment was lenient by Roman legion standards. Typically, the other men in their unit clubbed deserters to death, but clubbing wasn't necessary in Briton. Everyone knew that a Roman on his own without protection was at the mercy of the wild tribes. The chance that these three would make it to the Roman-held territories in the south was almost zero. More likely, tribesmen would take them and kill them in some horrible way. Patrols had found deserters who they had roasted alive slowly over campfires, other who they had skinned and tied down over an anthill.

The common wisdom among the ranks was that a banished man should kill himself at the first opportunity—cut open his veins with a sharp rock and sit outside the gate thanking the gods for an easy death. Suicide rarely happened of course; the strongest instinct of a coward was to run no matter what savage atrocities they had seen or heard about. It just wasn't in their cowardly heads to find an honorable end.

Centurion Marcus Metella stood at attention at the front of his century watching the proceedings. Ironic, he thought, that the prefect stands on the same spot they had used to flog the Britons to death the night before. The prefect talks of us representing civilization, he thought, but we can be just as brutal as the Brits. Maybe even worse; we do what we do in cold bold; at least the savages have their wild rage as an excuse.

It did not matter, he decided. We *believe* that we represent civilization and progress, and therefore we do.

95

The Brits *believe* they are fighting for their lands and for their freedom, therefore they do. Right and wrong doesn't matter here. There is no one to challenge either belief; no one to find the real motivations behind all this killing.

He watched as the former legionaries walked out the gate. They would find these three in a few days or weeks after the Brits had finished with them. These cowards would then perform their last duty for the legion—to shock their former comrades with the horror of their deaths. This is the ideal outcome for the prefect, the more terrible their deaths the better.

"The cowards serve us well by dying so miserably," he had once told Metella. "Our men are motivated to fight twice as hard after we find the remains of their friends. They almost welcome the quick and easy deaths they can find during a battle. Most importantly, Marcus, they don't blame us for the sorry end of their friends. It's the savages who get the blame. Everyone wins; except the cowards of course, who deserve nothing better."

He had nodded in enthusiastic agreement at the time. Prefect Gaius Lepidi was a hard man, a true soldier. He would sacrifice men without a moment's hesitation to win. He did whenever was necessary for the legion to be victorious. Metella admired him and his single-minded focus, everyone did. He kept them alive.

The centurion dismissed his men and walked to where the prefect was standing, intending to offer his support. He knew that despite the man's speech and his irrefutable logic, that the prefect would be feeling low. Cowardice was a dangerous and depressing subject for a fighting unit no matter how useful it was in motivating the men.

"Bad business, sir," he muttered sympathetically. "We're lucky there were so few this time. It was a vicious fight."

The older man nodded and began to move off towards his hut. The Centurion turned with him and followed at his side.

"We'll find the cowards soon," Lepidi predicted. "They ran from a battle that we were winning from the beginning. Imagine what would happen if they were in a fight that we were losing. These cowards have no sense of timing." He paused. "Timing is everything in life, Marcus."

Metella remained silent. Sometimes the prefect just wanted to talk, to voice his simple philosophies to another soldier, someone who understood.

"I want you to organize the patrols tomorrow, Marcus. I suspect the savages will be quick to accommodate us after their defeat at Wolf's Glen. Use a detachment of cavalry; I don't want any more casualties. Make sure that you bring the bodies back to the camp just the way you find them and put them on display immediately. The men can use a good object lesson after this last battle."

"I'm surprised there were only three," Lepidi repeated in a soft voice. "I thought more would run—all that insane screaming from their women... That's what gets to you, you know, the noise. It works its way inside your head and infects your brain with fear. We need to bring the drums closer to the fighting ranks...make some of our own noise to drown out the savages."

"The men appreciate your leadership, *Praefectus*," Metella replied, nodding. "We could have all been killed if you had not maintained discipline in the face of the women's charge. I wanted to turn and face them myself."

"Me too," the old man admitted, nodding his head, grateful for the support. Marcus Metella was more than just a subordinate, the prefect felt close to him, like a son. That was why he mentored him. Taking a protégé was a common practice in the legions. Most officers learned tactical and technical skills in the field under combat conditions, but there were always subtleties in any battle that needed explanation. Someday, Centurion Marcus Metella might replace him as the Legion's *praefectus castrorum*. That was the prefect's hope.

"May I discuss a private matter with you, Sir?" Metella asked carefully.

The General looked at him, surprised. Metella never asked for special favors; this was one of the reasons the general favored the man. A request for a private meeting could only mean a favor.

"Come inside, Centurion. I need some wine to wash the bad taste of cowardice out of my mouth."

Metella nodded and followed him inside. The general went quickly to the wine and poured them both a cup. They removed their swords and sat, comfortable with each other's company.

"I took a Brit woman, a girl really, out of the prisoner chain last night," Metella began slowly. "She struck me as I was walking by. The tribune had condemned her...racking...for killing six of our men. She was one of the women who flew at us from the west yesterday."

Lepidi looked at him strangely. "Why did you take her. Isn't racking enough of a punishment for you?"

The prefect didn't like long preambles. He also knew that Metella would not act so irrationally without a good reason. Taking a woman earmarked for execution for his private use was not appropriate behavior for an officer, especially one destined to become the *primus pilus*.

"Anyway, isn't there another scheduled for racking this morning?"

"My sergeant substituted her for the other. He was trying to protect me."

"Marcus..."

The word expressed his profound disappointment.

"Do I need to tell you that bad behavior by an officer can quickly lead to dissent among the ordinaries which could easily become a mutiny. It has happened before in Briton."

"No, I know."

"I presume you had a good reason for coming to me now," he added quietly in a serious and official tone.

Metella was his protégé. He had great hopes for the young man. But he was also a stickler for the rules.

"I want to cancel the racking, both. The girl scheduled to be racked is innocent and the girl I took can be more valuable to us in another way."

"Marcus...," the general said again.

"There was just something about her that struck me as different and, well, frankly, I wanted her. She is quite beautiful in a wild sort of way," Metella said honestly. There was no way he was going to lie to the old man even if it meant punishment.

"You were thinking with your cock..." Lepidi said sternly then added, "Not very smart behavior for a professional soldier, a future leader."

"Yes, you're right of course, but there was something more to this girl. I admit, I wanted to fuck her, but I also saw something in her that I couldn't explain, something

99

that I couldn't leave alone. I want to think I was following a hunch; that behind her hatred there was…understanding. She knew us somehow and I…I was curious to find out what she knew and how. Usually, these Brits show nothing but animal instinct. She was different."

Lepidi looked at him skeptically. The boy was rambling. It was easy to succumb to a manly lust then rationalize it later. He had seen it happen a thousand times. Fucking her was not important; it was the violation of discipline that bothered him. On the other hand, Lepidi thought, we are all men with natural urges. He didn't want men around him who were so disciplined that they could suppress every natural desire, he just wanted them to control themselves…to think before acting. This was why the Second Legion prospered under his tactical leadership—always the fewest number of casualties and the largest number of enemy deaths among all the legions in the North. He put thinking ahead of fighting.

"Well, were you right? Was she different?" the general prompted.

"She speaks Latin, Sir," Marcus answered simply. "I don't know how, but she speaks Latin perfectly. Not just a few words, true conversational Latin, and she understand us—how we fight, how we think. It's uncanny, Prefect. I felt as if I am speaking to another Roman when I speak to her."

The older man stared at him without comprehension.

"I don't understand," he said blankly. "How could a savage, here in the North, speak perfect Latin?"

"Apparently, she was a prisoner before. She must have listened to her guards talking and…learned. She is not willing to tell me how," Marcus added. "I guess we could interrogate her on this point, but…is it really that important…how she learned?"

Lepidi laughed. "She struck you while under a death sentence and refused to answer your questions!"

Metella had not offered up so many words in a year. He was usually as taciturn as the prefect.

"Why are we discussing this, Marcus?" he asked impatiently. "The problem here is your loss of control, your violation of discipline. If you really need the girl to relieve your pressure, I will give her to you. She is of no consequence; get her out of your system. Violating a regulation on the other hand, is a serious matter, as you well know."

The younger man remained quiet, ignoring the prefect's change in direction. He had no intention of turning this into a discussion of legion discipline.

"I have an idea, *Praefectus*, an idea that could help us win more victories against the savages with fewer losses." He stopped and waited a few seconds as he had seen the prefect do many times. "…But it is an idea that is far above my rank."

"Above your rank…?" the general was confused and frustrated trying to follow his protégé.

"Spit it out for Zeus' sake, Marcus," he growled angrily. "I'm in no mood for fucking games this morning. You came to ask me something, what is it?"

Metella settled back in his chair. The prefect's bluster didn't scare him. They had fought too many battles, seen too much together. He needed to lay out his proposal step-by-step so that the prefect could build a persuasive case for the other officers in his own mind, in his own way.

"The Second Legion fights well, Prefect. Yes, we have an occasional deserter, but for the most part, the legion is an extraordinary and devastating instrument of war, probably the best fighting unit in all of Briton. You have honed it to an extraordinarily sharp point," he paused again and lowered his voice, "But we cannot win here the way we fight. You know it, everyone knows it."

Lepidi frowned at him. This was dangerous, defeatist talk. They both needed to tread carefully.

"Yesterday was a perfect example. The local tribe set their women and children on us rather than accept defeat properly, rather than surrender. There are a thousand such villages ahead of us, all of whom are equally irrational, all of whom have sworn to defeat us at any cost. Yes, we lose only one legionary for every hundred savages we kill, but they have an infinite supply to draw from; we only have a trickle of inexperienced recruits to replace our casualties. Slowly but surely, they will wear us down."

He paused. They both knew that this talk was not politically correct, but the prefect also knew that the best ideas often bubbled up from below.

"So...?" he asked slowly. The question in his voice showed that he didn't dispute any of what Metella had said.

"We need allies or at least villages who will remain neutral. Every savage we convert to an ally or a neutral by negotiating a settlement will be a victory...perhaps not one with the same glory as one that is won in a bloody fight, but strategically..."

The older man continued to stare. There was a hard look in his eyes now.

"What do you know of strategy, Centurion? ...Or politics?" he asked sternly. "What right do you have to question the legion's approach, the legate's overall plan?"

"...Nothing and none, Gaius," Marcus answered in a determined voice. "I only know that whatever strategy we have, it's not working. It cannot work. These savages will never surrender, to us, we have all seen this time after time. It's not in them to surrender. We need to add diplomacy as a weapon. We need to negotiate before we fight. We can't wait until the Brits are conquered to apply some common sense to them."

He paused. This was daring talk for someone so low in the legion's hierarchy.

"We will all die here, Prefect, if we don't try something different. You are responsible for the legion's tactics...for winning battles. You are the one who actually wields the weapon that is the legion. Aren't you the appropriate person to bring this proposal to the legate?"

The older man poured another round of wine but remained silent. They both knew that what Metella just said was a convenient lie. Prefect Gaius Lepidi was in charge of battlefield tactics—military movements—negotiations were the province of the political commander, the *tribuni angusticlavii*, and his supporters in Rome. They owned the political arena. Soldiers like Gaius and the centurion were simply there to fight...and die as necessary.

Still...no one wanted Rome to lose the fight in Briton.

The centurion remained silent knowing that he had said enough.

"What exactly is your proposal, Marcus?" the prefect asked. He dealt in facts and certainties. This talk of politics was outside his area of expertise.

"Let me turn the slave girl to our purpose. She was with these Catuvellauni people in the battle, but I suspect she was not one of them. I believe the Catuvellauni took her in to fatten their lines for the coming battle with us. I think she convinced them to take her in.

"The Briton tribes are allied only by their hatred of Rome, nothing more. If I can turn her to our cause, she can speak for us to the other tribes. She can be part of our tactical weaponry. She can help us win bloodless victories. We can't do this if we can't communicate with the savages. She could be our voice."

Lepidi was listening intently now, his head down.

"All Britons who speak Latin are to be turned over to the theater command," the general said mechanically, "to help interrogate the prisoners we send back. How else can we gain the intelligence we need...? Those are our orders."

"Those translators serve no good purpose so far from the front line," Metella interrupted with blunt certainty. "It's here, at the front, that they are needed. We need to speak with the savages here, not back at headquarters after they have been defeated."

"We have our own translators for that purpose," Gaius countered.

"Not like this one," Marcus countered. "She speaks Latin fluently. She thinks in Latin. She understands the nuances, the intent of our words. She understands the way we think. But most importantly, Gaius, she hates us... That hatred is out in the open not hidden behind a mask of self-serving friendship like our other translators. Most of them know Latin because they want to collaborate with us. This means that before they say a single word, the

104

savages we face despise them. What Briton chief wants to speak with us through a traitor, a coward? Would you...?"

Gaius was silent for a moment.

"If she hates us so much, why would she serve as an intermediary?" he asked skeptically. "The legate thinks all of these savages are animals, incapable of intelligent communication, let alone diplomacy. He says publicly that we might need to kill every one of them before peace can be achieved."

"What do you think of that idea, Prefect?" Marcus asked softly.

"It's ridiculous, but no one cares what I think about the politics of this place. The legate listens to my tactical military advice because it allows him to win battles, but he keeps his own counsel with respect to matters of governance and politics. He has his own men for those purposes, men from Rome."

There was a note of frustration even rage in his voice that he was unable to hide.

"Speak to the legate, Prefect," Metella urged. "He'll listen to you; you are the only one capable of winning battles for him. Give me a month with the girl and..." he hesitated, "and the means to win her to our side against the savages."

Lepidi was immediately alert. His young protégé didn't just want support, he did want a favor.

"What 'means?'" he asked directly.

"I need absolute control over the thirty women destined for the slave block, the pretty ones."

He hesitated, knowing that the prefect must accept this part of his plan on faith

"I will return the investment a hundred-fold in no-cost victories, Prefect."

Lepidi looked at him with surprise and amusement. He had never known the centurion to be so bold with his ideas. Was this a good sign for the future or an indication of growing recklessness? He wondered. He knew it was important for him to determine which.

"You want us to invest the trophy slaves, the bulk of the legion's profits from the battle, in your scheme!" he asked gruffly, "…Anything else you want, Centurion?"

"Yes," Metella answered boldly, "I need the Princess Ailios, Caratacus's daughter, the one destined to be sent back to Rome."

Legionaries had found the princess in the Caratacus's family hut awaiting news of the battle at Wolf's Glen. They had taken her and her three retainers prisoner. The legion's commander intended to send her and her father back to Rome as trophies, symbols of the legion's victory. Since she was of royal blood, the emperor would probably marry her to a low-level Roman and give him some political office back in Briton. The emperor didn't like to spill royal blood.

"You think the legate is going to turn over the Catuvellauni princess to you? She is valuable to these palace-Romans for her title."

"It's a small value," Metella answered. "She's more valuable to us serving me in this plan. I need her to demonstrate to my slave that her loyalties are better placed with us than with the other tribes," Metella explained briefly.

"You think you can turn 'your slave' away from her own people?" the prefect asked guardedly, sipping his wine.

"No, she will never side fully with us. Her loyalty was with her family and her tribe which I believe, we

106

eliminated. But I can show her that shifting her emotional allegiance to the other Briton tribes is ill-advised. The Brits are not a nation. They don't fight us as a single people; they are a collection of selfish tribes each out for themselves. Once she sees this, I believe she will give us enough of her allegiance to satisfy our purpose."

He stopped talking and remained silent for several minutes allowing the old man time to think.

Finally, he couldn't wait any longer.

"It's worth a try, Prefect. What have we got to lose? Thirty slaves...? They are nothing. There are thirty-thousand comely Brit women awaiting our chains further north if we can succeed. Why not gamble with these few?"

"The legate is not going to authorize such a venture," the prefect said in a matter-of-fact tone. "He is watched too closely by Tetanus, his secretary. The man is a spy for those in Rome who want to keep the legate on a close leash. The legate won't even listen to such a proposal while Tetanus is keeping the minutes of his meetings. I cannot overcome that constraint; after all, I am only the legion's *praefectus castrorum*."

The centurion starred at him for several seconds, profoundly disappointed. He knew nothing of command politics. He had not had any idea there was a spy in the legate's tent. He nodded his head in sympathetic understanding. On the other hand, he knew that Lepidi loved to turn every discussion into a criticism of Rome, especially regarding to the interference of the Roman emissaries. He knew the prefect, perhaps better than he knew himself. A secretary from Rome, even one assigned to the legate, was not going to stand in the way of something the legate believed in, of something that helped the legion.

"Too bad," Metella answered sincerely. "I feel strongly that the girl was an opportunity for us to do more than fight and die. Too bad...we are confounded by one man...from Rome."

Lepidi nodded his agreement, "Yes, too bad, but don't get discouraged, such ideas are always welcome."

He turned dismissively towards the pile of scrolls on his table.

"Save the girl being racked, Marcus, and keep your Brit whore another few days," he said crisply as Metella was leaving, "then return her to the slave keepers. I don't want to hear any talk of unfairness from the ranks. I will smooth over your violation with the legate. I'll say the girl had some intelligence that we were trying to obtain by torturing her in private." He thought for a minute, "...so torture her some, will you."

"If anything changes regarding your proposal, I'll call you," he added as an afterthought.

Metella nodded and left. Lepidi was not a man he could push. He had listened to his arguments; now he needed to weigh them for himself and make his own decision.

***

The next day, latrine workers found the legate's secretary, Tetanus Amici Lepardo, dead, his throat slit from ear to ear, floating face down in the legate's personal latrine. The legate, assuming it was a man from the ranks, ordered the prefect to investigate and bring the guilty person to justice. The prefect turned the camp upside down, but never found the killer

His written report of the death of Tetanus Amici Lepardo, which the legate forwarded on to Rome, strongly supported the theory that a Brit, intent on killing the legate, had slipped over the stockade fence and killed the "beloved" secretary, who was using the legate's private latrine. It was a plausible explanation and the bureaucracy in Rome quickly moved on from the issue of Tetanus's murder. They were much more concerned with finding a suitable replacement for their spy as quickly as possible.

Metella found it an interesting coincidence that the Brit had killed the secretary only a day after Lepidi had voiced his concern about a spy in the legate's tent. He found it an even more interesting coincidence that the investigation commanded by Lepidi missed searching his tent and missed finding the slave girl he was keeping bound inside.

Two days later, a messenger formally summoned Centurion Marcus Metella to the prefect's tent. Lepidi and the legion's *tribunus laticlavius,* second in command and political advisor to the legate, Artimus Concerti, were present. The tribune was standing silently off to the side, observing.

Metella came to attention and saluted both senior officers smartly. Like most of the legion's officers, he had no respect for the tribunes whom he considered politicians hacks—his loyalty was to the prefect—but he did understand the need for a chain of command and for showing respect to those of higher ranks. The prefect would never stand for any breach of military etiquette especially during a formal meeting.

"The legate has approved your proposal, Centurion, to turn the Brit slave known as Xara to our purpose," he said without preamble. "He hereby grants you the power of *mortui vivos docent* (death teaches the living) over her and over thirty other female slaves of your choosing for five days. He further assigns you custody of the woman, Ailios, Princess, daughter of Caratacus, chief of the Catuvellauni."

The prefect glanced down at the scroll on his table. It obviously contained a written version of the orders he was now issuing verbally. Tribune Concerti was there to be sure that the prefect did not deviate from the script they had agreed.

"He has further assigned you the command of a *contubernium* (squad) specifically for the purpose of slave-keeping. You may choose the members of this unit. Sergeant Spurius Vipsanius will serve as you second-in-command for the duration of this assignment. You are hereby relieved of your current assignment."

This was a significant bonus, Marcus thought. Viper was comfortable executing orders for punishment, which Metella knew would be necessary. Ordinary soldiers would have been too squeamish, too hesitant to do what was necessary. The sergeant had no such compunctions.

"Are there any questions?"

"None, Sir," Metella answered, saluting smartly. He knew that the prefect had guaranteed the success of his plan with his career. This, Metella reasoned, was another reason the tribune was attending the meeting and the prefect was being so correct—he was here as a witness. Metella had no doubt that despite the prefect's immense value to the legion, the legate would force him into retirement if this plan went badly. Thirty slaves was a

110

substantial investment for the legion; they would need a scapegoat, and he was too low on the totem pole to serve this purpose if it failed; it had to be the prefect. This was just the way things were done.

The old man leaned forward and spoke softly to him, too low for the tribune to hear.

"*Audaces fortuna iuvat* (fortune favors the bold), Marcus, but boldness alone doesn't guarantee success. This is your opportunity; do not fail me or yourself, but most importantly, do not embarrass either of us."

Metella saluted and walked back to his tent. Xara was where he had left her, tied naked over a rough bench by her wrists and ankles to its four legs. He found the gag and the ass hook viper had given him then he undressed and sat straddling the bench near the girl's head. Without rushing, he braided her hair with a rawhide cord, greased the asshook, then inserted it into her anus and tied it to the cord. He pulled hard and her head came up, her face inches from his scrotum.

"During interrogation, one of the Catuvellauni woman disclosed that your name was Xara and that you are of the Taexali Tribe, now extinct for failing to bow to Roman authority."

Her eyes were on his cock and his growing erection. It was obvious that he intended to fuck her again as he had been doing for days, this time in the mouth.

"So, you now know my name, *ignavus*. Do you think that gives you some power over me?"

"No. My power comes from your bondage, from the whip in my kit, from my ability to best you in personal combat. Soon it will come from your loyalty to your friends, to your people, to your need to survive if you want to kill more Romans."

111

"You speak in riddles, *ignavus*. Are you drunk? Just get on with your coward's fuck. One day, I will cut off your cock and put it in your mouth for you to suck."

"Perhaps you will," he answered quietly, "but until then, it's you who will do the sucking and me who will do the fucking."

He pushed the rawhide covered ring into her mouth behind her front teeth then tied it behind her neck. Slowly, with her drool soaking the top of the bench, he inserted his cock deep into her throat then began to gently and slowly pull it in and out so she could breathe. He put his hands behind to balance then leaned back, luxuriating in the feel of her throat muscles tightening and loosening, in the desperate flicking of her tongue on his penis.

He would fuck her in a while, but for now he just wanted to enjoy her subjugation. Soon, if all went according to plan, she would submit to him, and their work could begin.

Chapter Seven - Mercy

Ailios, daughter of Caratacus, and princess of the Catuvellauni people looked down at the girl kneeling at her feet. She was trembling, her body shaking as if from some terrible fever. Ailios let her wait for a long time, enjoying the power.

She sat in a fine chair, clothed in a red robe, under an overhand made of white cloth; the Romans had supplied all of these items and more, thereby indicating that she had royal authority over the Catuvellauni prisoners, specifically the other thirty women in their section. Her father was still suffering from his wounds, delirious with the infection that had developed after the battle. Her mother was dead, killed with the first wave of screeching women at Wolf's Glen, as were her three brothers.

It wasn't clear what the romans intended for the Princess Ailios. Most likely, if her father recovered, they would send the chief and his daughter to Rome to face the emperor's justice. At that time, the emperor might have them killed or grant them status as his vassals, to govern a part of the new Roman Briton under Rome's thumb. The fact that two family members had survived made this outcome likely if Caratacus agreed as it gave the emperor leverage. If the chief did not survive his wounds, the emperor would probably enslave her as a curiosity—the beautiful princess of the Catuvellauni—or just put her up for sale with the others destined for sexual service.

There were any number of possible outcomes for Princess Ailios, but until they powers that be decided her fate, she would remain the figurehead leader of the tribe.

"You have been seen giving comfort to the enemy," Ailios said quietly, just loudly enough for the girl to hear. "What have you got to say for yourself?"

Witnesses had seen the girl near the back of the slave pen sucking one of the guards' cocks after licking his balls like an adoring pet. She was young, perhaps nineteen or twenty; Princess Ailios was only a year or two older.

"I was hungry, Mistress. He offered me bread to…and, well, I was hungry."

"We are all hungry," Ailios replied. "Do you think if we all agreed to suck Roman cock, they would feed us better?"

The girl didn't say anything for a time. She was trembling with fear, but also angry. Ailios, as Caratacus's daughter, was the recognized leader of the tribe, but the tribe no longer existed, except as a defeated group of Roman slaves. It wasn't the bread that had compelled her to do what she had done; it was the Roman. He was nice to her, kind. She had offered him her mouth to repay him for his kindness. What was wrong with that?

"Isn't that our fate now, Mistress," she said bravely. "Haven't the Romans chosen us in this pen for sexual service? Won't we all be sucking Roman cock soon? Forgive me for saying, but perhaps even you, Mistress, if our chief dies."

It was true. The Romans had separated the attractive girls from the other prisoners and designated them for sexual service. Ailios nodded her head in agreement.

"You are right—we might all be fucking Romans soon—but your timing is all wrong. At this moment, while my father is recovering from his wounds, I rule the Catuvellauni, and my clear order was no fraternization

114

with the enemy. For disobeying that order, I sentence you to death by strangulation."

The girl looked up in surprise. Princess Ailios had the authority to enforce their laws, but not to destroy Roman property. The girl was a Roman slave...the legal property of the state by right of conquest. Damaging or destroying state property was a crime.

"You...you cannot do that Princess. I...I...am the property of Rome. You don't have the..."

Princess Ailios nodded and two of her Amazonian attendants grabbed the girl's arms while a third slipped a rope garrote around her neck and began to pull.

"You might be right," Ailios said as the other girls from the pen watched in horror, "but you will not be here to see it."

Everyone watched as her lips turned blue and her eyes bulged. Ailios had told the garroter to strangle her slowly as an example to the other women.

"I want them all to see what happens to those who disobey me. I want them to feel her pain, to watch as life slowly leaves her body."

It was a cruel death, one that seemed to go on forever. When she finally expired, they carried her naked body in the center of the pen and left it. In the morning, the Romans collected it for the trash. On the prefect's personal order, there were no repercussions, which implicitly gave Princess Ailios the power of life and death over everyone in the slave pen.

***

Centurion Marcus Metella took command of the thirty slaves destined for sexual service the next day. The

115

centurion he relieved read the orders carefully; his duty was to protect the princess and the other beauties in the pen from any violation, a role he took seriously.

"You know we have the Princess Ailios inside. She is the daughter of Caratacus. If he lives, the commander will send her back to Rome for trial. I should probably confirm this order with the legate."

Metella nodded agreeably.

"If you like. If you think the legate made a mistake in his order, you should go and check with him."

The centurion looked up at him for a moment then stepped back.

"No need, Centurion, the legate doesn't make mistakes."

Metella turned towards Viper and nodded. Viper and the men of his new "special unit" organized the twenty-nine into three coffles and marched them to an isolated pen in the corner of the camp. The cavalry had been being using it for some of their horses until this morning. The slave-girl Xara arrived in chains separately causing a stir among the others as to where she had been all this time. One of Ailios attendants asked her, but Xara had refused to say anything.

Xara knew the princess, Caratacus had introduced them. Since then, they had had an unspoken understanding to ignore each other. Princess Ailios knew that the Taexali girl had infatuated her father with her lean hard body and her astonishing knife skills. Xara knew that her mother's embarrassment and her father's lust had put Princess Ailios unfairly in the middle, and she tried to keep their love affair as discrete as possible. It wasn't that a chief could not or should not have a mistress, it was that he spent all his free time with Xara, avoiding his family.

116

Metella entered the horse pen around midday and stood on a low wooden platform in the center of the open area. He spoke loudly for all to hear, but it was obvious that he was addressing himself mostly to Xara.

"I have an important message for these slaves," he said to Xara in Latin. "If you want to help them and yourself, you will translate my words."

He turned to face the crowd. It was obvious that he expected Xara to obey.

"My name is Centurion Marcus Metella," he began. "The reason you are here is to prepare you for execution for rebellion. You have been convicted of this crime by written order of *Legatus Legionis* Senatorus Plecio, commander of the Ninth Legion."

It was true, as a formality for enslavement, the legate had condemned all the Catuvellauni prisoners to death. Metella turned back to Xara and waited for her to translate, but she remained stubbornly silent. If she continued to resist him, his plan would fail before it began.

"Roman law," he continued, trying to hide his disappointment, "imposes the penalty of crucifixion on anyone who engages in rebellion against the empire."

He turned to Xara again, but she stayed silent.

"However, in his mercy, *Legatus Legionis* Senatorus Plecio, has authorized me to grant each of you *misericordia* (mercy) if the chief of the Catuvellauni, Caratacus the First, now represented by his daughter, the Princess Ailios, formally surrenders. A Roman commander in the field has the authority to commute this death sentence to enslavement-for-life when the enemy surrenders and requests pardon for their crimes.

"Our glorious Commander, who is also the Provincial Governor of this 12th Province of Briton, has agreed to commute your death sentence if we receive this formal surrender from reigning Catuvellauni authority, the Princess Ailios."

He nodded to the Princess acknowledging her position.

"She simply needs to ask and *misericordia* will be granted."

The twenty-nine women stared at him without understanding. Xara, who was struggling to distance herself from the centurion, remained silent. Marcus turned back to face her.

"I must receive the Princess's formal surrender by tomorrow morning. If I do not, we will begin to carry out the crucifixions as required by Roman law."

Xara stared at him silently, refusing to speak. After a while he shrugged and walked away apparently indifferent. In fact, he was devastated. If Xara maintained her stubborn silence and refused to translate the demand, then his plan would fail. Everything depended on her and Princess Ailios playing the roles he had defined for them. Viper and his special unit were waiting for him at the gate.

"Do we really need their formal surrender, Centurion?" Viper asked, curious. "They are savages whom we have enslaved. These thirty will make the legion a lot of money. Why is it any more complicated than that? Why would we want to crucify them?"

Marcus turned towards him ignoring his questions.

"Have your men prepare a cross. We will crucify one of the prisoners in the morning. Do you understand, Sergeant?"

Viper nodded.

"There will be no disciplining of these slaves today. I want them treated well, supplied with water, food, clothing, and the means to bathe. Maintain good security, but there will be no whips in the pen today."

Viper looked even more confused.

"We are going to treat them kindly before we crucify them?" he asked.

"I want to remind them that life can be sweet," Marcus answered, "before we show them the alternative. You understand?"

"Of course, Centurion," but it was obvious that he did not.

Again, with the mystery, Viper was thinking. Fucking officers! Still, guard duty and executions were light assignments. Other soldiers were already transporting Catuvellauni prisoners south to the slave depot at Rumabo This assignment had spared him from that dangerous job.

Inside the pen the women were gathering around Xara. It was apparent that the girl had kept her knowledge of Latin a secret in the village, a secret that Marcus had just revealed by addressing her in the hated Roman tongue. They knew that the centurion had said something that she had refused to translate. Despite her resolution not to cooperate with the Romans, it was going to be hard for her to maintain her silence now.

Princess Ailios, unlike the others, seemed to have no interest in a translation of the Roman's words. She and her retinue had moved to a corner of the new pen and set up her overhand and a protective cordon.

It has started, Marcus thought, noting the movements of the prisoners. The observation made him feel slightly better about his speech. It is not happening exactly the way he intended but.... The pressure on the girl to provide detailed information and to interpret what he had said will be intense especially once the executions start. The open question now was Princess Ailios. Would she react in the way he expected? Too much integrity on her part would ruin his plan as would too little. He needed her to continue to remain as aloof and as unconcerned as she had been, at least for a while longer while he backed Xara into a corner.

***

Xara sat back against the rough-hewn logs of the pen's enclosure. It was hot and the only shade came from the wooden overhang that ran along the back wall of the stable. Several girls were bathing in the horse trough with the water the Romans had provided; others were busy trying on the cloth they had supplied. Xara marveled at how much a good meal, a bath, and a length of cloth had improved the mood inside the pen.

If they only knew what was going to happen in the morning. Do I have the right to keep it from them, she wondered?

As for herself, she had simply washed quickly and tied the wrap low on her hips leaving her upper torso bare. Modesty in a female slave pen was a ridiculous self-deception.

Around noon one of the girls, Tegan, approached her.

"Greetings, Xara," she began in a friendly voice.

Tegan had been engaged to one of the village's most powerful sub-chiefs. Xara had seen the Romans hoist the

120

man up a tree at Wolf Glen. He had died well, she remembered.

"Tegan," Xara answered cautiously.

She had nothing against this girl who, like most of the others in the village had mostly ignored her during her time with the Catuvellauni. Once Caratacus had declared her an ally in his fight against the Romans and implicitly identified her as his mistress, she had acquired a special status; the men and the women of the village had avoided her after that.

Their shunning was understandable—she was an outsider and an escaped slave, someone who had spent time with the hated Romans. No one ever asked if she could speak Latin and she had never volunteered the information not even to Caratacus. Nor had anyone ever asked her if she had hurt or killed anyone during her escape. The fact that she had killed the camp's legate, the commander of the Ninth Legion, Lucius Flaccus, during her escape was also a secret.

"The others," Tegan began, "have asked me to speak with you about what the Roman said to us today. He seemed to be directing himself to you as if you understood their language. They, the other women, would like to know what he said."

Tegan let out a sigh and began to finger-comb her long red hair. It was as if she could relax now that she had delivered the message. Xara stared her then looked over at the other women. They were glancing nervously in her direction, waiting for her response.

"Did he say where they were going to send us...somewhere warm I hope, she said smiling? I enjoy the summer." The girl seemed to have recovered from the death of her fiancée, the destruction of her tribe, and her

121

enslavement. Xara marveled at her ability to adapt to her new circumstance; she would make an excellent slave.

"Maybe they will send us to Rome. I have heard that Rome is a city of baths; that everyone bathes naked in public; that slaves in the bath can be...well, fucked anytime by any Roman citizen." The girl paused to blush. "You think that's true, Xara? Someone told me that Romans order their slaves to suck their cocks whenever they feel the urge; that if they don't, they whip them until they scream in pain. Is this true? The Roman whipped you for striking him that first night. What were you thinking when you did that? Did his whipping hurt?"

The girl continued to babble on without waiting for or caring about the answers. Xara got the distinct impression that she might enjoy sucking cock and being whipped.

"Someone else told me that Romans train young girls to pull their carts like horses; that their arms are tied up behind...and that they use reins to steer...and a long whip to make the girls run faster..."

There was a spark of curiosity her eyes. Xara had the impression that Tegan would also enjoy being a Roman pony girl for a while, that she would protest everything done to her in Rome but secretly revel in the excitement of a submissive life.

Many of them probably think this way, Xara realized suddenly. They must believe that their beauty makes them special, that it protects them from the pain and drudgery of a slave's existence. They see life with the Romans as a kind of sexual adventure, a release from the natural conservatism of the tribe.

"I'm not sure that I believe everything the others are saying," Tegan added, "but Rome sounds, well, exciting don't you think?" she paused and looked over at Xara. "I know that we are just slaves, but I've been told that a slave in Rome lives better than a chief in Briton...or a princess. Maybe what has happened to us is not so terrible...at least for us, you know, the pretty ones."

"They are going to kill us," Xara said bluntly, annoyed by her childish rationalizing. "They are going to crucify us. It's the traditional method of execution for rebels. We will all end our days nailed to a Roman cross."

She wanted to end the girl's silly prattle. Tegan stopped playing with her hair and stared at her without comprehension.

"We are not rebels," she said, stunned, "...And why would they want to kill us? We're valuable. Everyone knows that."

"Anyone who fights Rome is a rebel, subject to crucifixion," Xara explained. "They pardon some and sentence them to enslavement but not all."

"Why...why would they do that?" Tegan asked. "We are their slaves now...their property. Why would they destroy their own property? It makes no sense. I'm still a maiden," she added with emphasis, as if that fact alone made her invulnerable.

"The Roman centurion said that their law requires the tribe's chief or his legal heir and representative to surrender formally." Xara pointed in the direction of Princess Ailios. "If he does not receive a formal surrender from the princess, he will assume that we are all unrepentant enemy fighters and execute us."

The girl was having trouble following the explanation. It flew in the face of her more comfortable logic, a logic that she shared with the rest of the group. Xara knew that this kind of optimism was contagious.

123

"Why would they give us food and cloth if they were going to...?" Tegan reminded her in a pleading voice. "Would they give us water to bathe with if they were going to kill us? You're wrong, Xara. You misunderstood what he said. Where did you learn to speak their words?"

She desperately needed Xara to give her another translation another version of what Metella had said. She wanted the terror of the last few days to end. Before Wolf Glen things were simple for Tegan—get married, fuck her husband, have his children, and live the life of an important village wife. The Roman victory had destroyed that future, disorienting her to the point where nothing and everything made sense. Tegan, Xara realized, would be happy with her slavery if it provided her with stability.

"The Romans want the princess to surrender for her father," Xara said more gently, trying to soften and simplify the message for the girl. "If she refuses, they will kill us as examples like they did to the wounded men a Wolf's Glen. The fact that we are destined for sexual slavery makes the example of our deaths more compelling."

Tegan looked at her then abruptly stood up and walked back to the other women. Xara watched as they consumed her news. Many of the women were staring at her with threatening looks as if she was the source of this new terror. Xara stared back indifferently. Her strong instinct had always been to stay quiet, hidden in the background, but Metella had made this impossible by singling her out during his speech. Why had he done that, she wondered? Her knowledge of their language made no difference anymore. She was a slave. They were all slaves—Roman property—or at least they would be if the princess asked for mercy.

The princess...

Xara had no love or even respect for the girl. It was Princess Ailios who had organized the women for the battle and ordered the children into their ranks. Xara had known from the beginning that the Romans would not turn to fight the women; she had tried to tell Caratacus this that last day, but he just assumed that their legate or their prefect would not sit by and watch his women slaughter their men. He had been wrong; he didn't know how ruthless the Romans could be.

Of all those in the Catuvellauni village, she was the only one who knew that the Romans were savages dressed in fine cloth and armor.

She turned away from the women's stares. Her task now was to escape. She had no time for the petty squabbles of Catuvellauni women or for the politics of a princess without a kingdom. She had escaped the romans before, and she could do it again. It will be harder this time thanks to the centurion's attention and the resulting loss of her precious anonymity, but she could do it, she must do it.

There were no other options. There was no compromise with the Romans. They were wild dogs, killing and enslaving everyone they met. She knew them well from the slave depot at the Rumabo Imperium; she knew the evil that was in their hearts. The soldiers had taught her more than their language, they had shown her their true nature. She could still see the look of surprise and evil reprisal on the face of Lucius Flaccus as she strangled him. His arrogance knew no bounds, not even death.

She had known that Flaccus wanted to fuck her the moment their eyes met. The centurion, Metella, was more difficult to read and more dangerous. He had whipped her to within an inch of her life; fucked her so hard that she had had lost control of herself, climaxing like a gutter-dog, but Metella had also spoken to her as if she were a real person. No Roman had ever done that before.

She had not told him anything about her time at Rumabo of course--they were mortal enemies, she would never volunteer any information to him--but their time together had been interesting, interesting and, well, interesting.

***

Towards evening, one of Ailios retainers summoned her to the corner where Princess Ailios was resting. Xara had no choice but to obey. She stopped at a respectful distance, but she didn't kneel; she was unsure of the protocol one used for a royal in a Roman slave pen. Three strong-looking girls surrounded her. They functioned as both servants and guards. After a time, Ailios looked up and gestured at Xara to come closer.

"You are the bitch who my father fucked like a dog, correct?"

Xara didn't answer.

"And now you speak for the Roman dogs...?" she continued.

Xara bristled. She wasn't afraid of Ailios but after so much time in the village, she had learned to be cautious around the royal child.

"Yes, Princess, I translated what the centurion said today for the others," she answered respectfully, "but I don't speak *for* the Romans."

126

Ailios stared at her with obvious disdain for several long seconds.

"There is not much difference between the two roles, is there?" she asked imperiously. There were a few snickers from her attendants.

"How did a whore like you come to speak their tongue?"

"I am no whore, Princess."

Ailios shrugged.

"I was held by Romans in the south after they captured me at Devana, after they slaughtered my people, the Taexali. I thought that learning their language would help me escape."

"Ah...," Ailios said, nodding. "Why didn't you tell us that you could speak their language when my father found you cowering in the swamp?"

She didn't wait for an answer.

"I've been told that you now fuck one of their officers...that you hungrily suck on his cock whenever it grows large."

Xara stared down at her feet and remained silent. She was right—Caratacus had saved her and given her, a stranger, refuge. She had owed him the truth; she should have told him that she understood Latin. Perhaps, she could atone for that error now...

"I was a Taexali maiden. The Romans killed my parent, slaughtered my people, and took me prisoner. I learned Latin by listening to the Roman soldiers. They had put me with their dogs and let me lie at their feet at night. I escaped when one of their officers took me outside the camp to rape me. Your father, Caratacus, took me to his bed after he rescued me. I could hardly refuse. I fought with the Catuvellauni...you saw me fight. After the Romans made me a prisoner, I struck the centurion, the one who spoke to us today. He tortured me in reprisal and raped me while he was doing it."

The princess snorted. She didn't believe the explanation, or she didn't want to accept it. Xara knew that under different circumstances, Ailios would have had her punished for allowing an enemy to use her sexually. She had seen it happen before; she had seen loose girls punished to set a good example for the others.

"A Catuvellauni woman would have found a way to deny the Roman access to her cunt," Ailios confirmed angrily. "But then again, you are a Taexali and not a true Catuvellauni woman, are you?"

She didn't wait for an answer.

"It doesn't matter, we will deal with your whoring and your treachery in good time. Perhaps some time staked out in the pigs' pen will remind you of where your loyalties belong."

In the past, the threat would have been real and fearsome. For serious sexual offenses, the Catuvellauni often stripped the offender naked and staked her out in a pig pen. The experience of laying with the pigs often caused madness. Even now, here in the slave pens, Ailios could command the remnants of the tribe towards a terrible vengeance. The princess sat back, seemingly content now that she had flexed the muscle of her remaining power.

"From now on you will tell me and only me what the Roman says. I will decide what information I communicate to the others. I will decide how we respond to the Romans, not you."

Xara felt her anger rising and she struggled to keep it hidden. She had killed or severely wounded six

128

formidable Romans in the battle. How many had the princess killed? She had not conspired with the Roman centurion, only translated what he had said. But antagonizing Ailios wouldn't help anyone.

"Yes, Princess," she answered meekly then continued to explain what the centurion had said, happy to have it off her shoulders and on Ailios's.

"The Roman wants your formal surrender, Princess. He says that Roman law requires that you ask for mercy on behalf of the tribe before he can accept our surrender. He says the lack of your surrender will force him to execute all of us here."

Xara paused and let her head fall forward. The princess was right; she had no standing in the Catuvellauni tribe. Who was she to be speaking to royal blood this way? Her only credential was that the chief fucked her.

"The Romana are trying to frighten us," Ailios declared haughtily. "They are afraid of us. They are afraid we will rise up and eat their fucking hearts."

Xara couldn't believe what she was hearing. She wondered if she should speak up...the Roman's threat was real, she knew it. She had to do something.

"I know you would rather fight on, Princess Ailios," she said respectfully, "but I can assure you that this Roman means what he says. We will all die here on the cross unless you surrender. There is no dishonor in this. The Catuvellauni people fought like demons. The battle of Wolf's Glen will be the stuff of legends and songs for generations to come. Dying here is this animal pen serves no purpose."

The blood rose in Ailios' face, and she stood up, enraged.

"Who are you? You are nothing but a miserable outsider, a cunt, a nobody, a...a...to tell me what serves the purpose of our tribe?" She was so angry that she was stumbling over her words. "You are nothing, you are less important than my shit...NOTHING! Homeless with no tribe, no family! My father was mortally wounded defending our people. He would expect his women to follow him, to sacrifice themselves. I don't take advice from Romans, and I certainly don't take it from the cum-filled, defiled mouth of a whore. My father was foolish to give refuge to such a low person as you."

Xara had heard enough.

"Please, listen to me Princess Ailios. I spent several days in this man's hands; I know him. He will do what he says. Do all these women have to die to uphold the honor of your family? Your father sent thousands of women and children into a battle that we could not win. He ended the Catuvellauni people by that decision. Was that honorable?"

The Princess took a step back. The very idea that someone so low would speak to her this way was beyond her imagination. Two of her attendants stepped forward, closer to Xara, but the Princess held up her hand while she collected herself.

"If it were possible, I would have you staked out for the pigs for speaking to me this way," she hissed. "Since we have no pigs, perhaps I will just have you strangled...very slowly."

Xara had a moment of regret that she had not been able to talk sense to this girl, but she didn't back down, she had lived with terror for years. She understood the need all Britons including Ailios had for revenge, but this was different. There was no revenge to be gained here

130

against the Romans, no way to achieve honor in defeat. This was a useless, senseless sacrifice, like the order Caratacus had given to have the women and children launch a diversionary attack. Ailios's resistance now would mean nothing, accomplish nothing.

"If I die, Princess, I have vowed to take at least one Roman with me, have you taken the same oath?" Xara said boldly then turned and walked away leaving the hissing Princess Ailios staring at her bare back.

Chapter Eight - Mercy Denied

Xara spent the rest of the day huddled in a corner of the horse pen, watching the rest of the trophy slaves enjoy their "gifts." She knew what the Roman Metella was doing. She had spent enough time with him to understand that he was no part-time soldier. His purpose was to win this war with the tribes, to bring all of Briton under the Roman heel.

He knew that Caratacus's daughter, the Princess Ailios, would never accede to his demand that she surrender in her father's name. He knew that her resistance would split the women into two camps—those who remained loyal to Caratacus and his royal family, and those who wanted to live. There would be many who would refuse to die so horribly for the honor of a royal family that no longer had a tribe to rule.

But why, she wondered? Why does the centurion care if the tribe remains loyal to Caratacus and his daughter or not? "…And what have I got to do with his plan," she asked herself aloud. Why did he reveal my secret, why does he want the tribe to know that I speak Latin? And why is he pushing me into this corner, forcing me to make this impossible choice

Her mind kept posing unanswered questions, but her body was remembering something else. Her time with Metella had not been all bad. He was not the lover that Caratacus was…he was better. He knew where and when to touch her; he knew how to be rough with her without being unnecessarily cruel; he knew how to use her fear and her pain to bring her to a state of arousal and orgasm that Caratacus, for all his skills, had never been able to achieve.

She was still his prisoner, still his slave, and she still hated all Romans including him, but there was something special about Metella. She fell off to sleep thinking about his cock in her mouth, how it had felt to be...

The centurion returned the horse pen the next morning and climbed onto the wooden platform. He waited patiently as Viper's troops rousted the thirty women, including Princess Ailios and pushed them to the center.

"What answer does the Princess give me?" he asked, again speaking directly to Xara.

She stared at him defiantly for a long time then answered him *in Latin* in a clear voice.

"The Princess surrenders, Master, and begs Roman mercy."

Metella nodded and smiled; it was obvious to him that Xara was lying, but this was exactly what he had hoped she would do. She was personally involved now, invested in the outcome of his little drama.

Princess Ailios was standing on the side looking belligerent. Metella was pleased—he had his translator, who was now also the *de facto* spokesperson for the group. She was thinking for them, making the decisions that the princess should be making. This was real progress, he thought. The next step for him was to shift her loyalties or at least reorienting them.

"Very well, ask her to fall to her knees and publicly beg for Roman mercy," he ordered.

Xara stood motionless for a moment then turned towards the princess.

133

"The Roman centurion asks that you to kneel before him as a gesture...of acceptance and friendship, Princess," she said reasonably, trying to avoid the confrontation between the Roman and the princess that now seemed inevitable.

The princess turned away from her ignoring the request.

"He will crucify every one of us if you do not surrender," Xara shouted for everyone to hear. "All you need to do, Princess, is acknowledge the fact that we have surrendered, that we are prisoners of Rome, that we are their slaves.

"This is our current reality, princess. It does not mean, however, that we need to give up. We can escape and continue to fight if we surrender now; we cannot continue to fight if we are dead!"

The girls in the crowd were panicking, looking from Xara to Ailios wondering what was happening. They did not understand Xara's exchange with Metella, they only understood what she had said to Ailios. It was Xara disclosure that their crucifixion was imminent, however, that got their attention.

"You are the only slave here, bitch," the princess shot back. "The sacred honor of the Catuvellauni people is at stake. I will never kneel before a Roman pig, and neither will I allow any of my people to kneel."

Xara turned back towards Marcus and smiled, trying to hide the venom in her exchange with Ailios.

"The Princess Ailios humbly asks that she be allowed to surrender tomorrow, Sir. Today is a holy day for the Catuvellauni. No tribal business can be conducted...today."

Marcus admired Xara's spontaneous creativity. He turned to Viper.

"Pick out one of the girls, Sergeant, and crucify her. Do not use nails or break any of her bones; use only ropes. I want her to live until sunrise tomorrow."

He turned back to Xara.

"The princess has until tomorrow morning to kneel before me, Xara. I feel, however, that she, you, and everyone here needs to understand my serious intent. Tomorrow, you will translate exactly what I say, or you will be the one on the cross. Do you understand?"

He waited until Xara nodded then he stepped down. On the way out the gate, he stopped and whispered further orders to Viper, pointing at Xara and then at Tegan, the girl who had approached her yesterday. Xara knew there would be no appeal or reversal of his death sentence. This was the way Romans made their point.

Xara stood frozen as Viper walked past her and grabbed Tegan's arm, pulling her out of the crowd. She began to scream and struggle as those around her stepped back. The two soldiers following behind Viper grabbed Tegans arms and lifted her off the ground, carrying her kicking and screaming to the other side of the pen's fence. There, other soldiers had started to assemble a cross from wood they carried in their wagon. The pen's gate closed and the women hesitantly walked to the fence to watch, numbed into silence by the sudden turn of events. Ailios stood staring at Xara with daggers in her eyes.

Viper's men worked quickly with practiced efficiency, first stripping Tegan of her slave cloth then forcing her naked body atop the cross. Two men held her arms in position while a third held her sklim ankles; a fourth soldier tied her wrists to the heavy wood with a

135

thick rope. Two others worked with a pick and a shovel to dig a hole for the cross.

Xara knew from past experience that all of their actions were calculated. They knew exactly what to do— they knew at what angle her arms needed to hang to achieve the greatest pain for the longest time; they knew the thickness of rope would hold her weight without cutting into her skin and allowing her to bleed to death; they knew the proper height above the ground to maximize the effect of her suffering on witnesses. Crucifixion was a Roman specialty. Done right, it kept a healthy man or woman in excruciating agony for a long time without any need for gore or blood or the screams rent from a victim by a professional torturer. In most cases, the exhausted victim eventually died from lack of air as their chest muscles, no langer capable of exanding, crushed their lungs and slowly strangled them. Sometimes, a stroke or heart attack mercifully finished them. If the person being cruxified lapsed into a irreversible coma, the disappointed Romans would spear them to make room for another victim.

Xara remembered one particularly cruel "maximum pain" cruxifixion in Rumabo when the soldiers used nails hammered into the man's wrists and feet to increase his pain from the suspension. They laughed as his screams made the dogs and her, who was laying with the dogs, restless. When his pain eventually trasformed into numbness, one of the soldiers in the execution detail used a heavy club to break his legs. He continued to scream for another hour.

Xara's eyes focused back on the helpless Tegan who was now too terrified to scream. She just kept snapping her head from side to side, pleading with her torturers to show her mercy. Xara knew that that the Romans assigned such duty rarely showed mercy. They were inured to the horrors of the cross. For the most part, Roman soldiers were peasents turned into ruthless automitons by the legion's harsh discipline and by officers who were often latent sadists.

The Centurion had ordered ropes, she remembered, watching them tie the girl's wrists and ankles. She knew what "ropes" meant—he wanted her to die from strangulation, and he wanted it to last, to take a full day. Nails would have been quicker, nails would have sent her into shock in a few hours as the metal slowly ripped open her limbs. He wanted Tegan to suffer a long time, just as he had wanted her to suffer when he stretched her on the *arcus-atrox*. Metella might not be a sadist in that he had a purpose for his attrocities, but he was cruel...

The men at the cross stood up, done with their gruesome bondage, and Viper walked casually to the diggers lambasting them for taking so long to finish digging the hole. He walked back to Tegan and stared down at her naked body now undulating wildly on the wood, twisting in a vain attempt to escape the ropes. Xara knew exactly what the sergeant was thinking—that this was a waste, that a luscious piece of meat like Tegan should be used for sex then sent to the slave block, not sacrificed for some reason that only Metella knew.

Xara felt the same—what was Metella doing crucifying this girl? He might be a cruel devil, but he was also a disciplined Roman devil and disciplined Roman's didn't do things without a reason. What did he hope to accomplish?

She watched the girl's struggle. She could tell from the way she was moving that she would have been an excellent lover, a genius with a man's cock. There was a certain bending motion in her writhing, a certain look on her face that confirmed to Xara that she would have welcomed submission. Most of those who were passive under torture were also passive during sex and during punishment. Tegan would have been different, she would have been special.

The man digging the hole called out to Viper and he nodded. Viper gave the order and the four legonaries loittering nearby lifted the heavy cross upright and set it roughly into the new hole facing the horse pen. Tegan screamed as the cross hit bottom and the weight of her body pulled on her arms. She twisted frantically trying to relieve the sudden compression on her chest.

Xara continued to watch, feeling guilty. Perhaps she should have remained silent when Metella asked his question. She had never gotten used to crucifixions, to the sight of someone suffering and dying in public view. Death, with all its humiliating indignities, should be a private thing. It was even worse to watch a woman suffer. In Rumabo, it had been rare for a slave, especially a valuable slave like Tegan, to commit an act that called for crucifixion. Usually the punishment was much simpler—a flogging or branding.

This is madness, she thought! The world around her had gone mad.

On viper's order, the soldiers untied Verna's legs which were about a foot off the ground. Xara had seen this before as well; it allowed the victim to grap the rough sides of the cross with her legs and feet. It gave the victim the false hope that she could hold herself up. There was no salvation from the agony of crucifiction—everyone suffered horribly and eventually died in terrible pain. The only question was "how long?"

Leaving her legs unbound, Xara suddenly realized, also meant that the Roman soldiers would have easy access to her cunt. This was what the devil Metella had whispered to Viper as he was leaving. He had given him and his men permission to fuck her as she hung from the wood.

She had also seen this before; she had seen woman on the cross franticly and unashamedly wrap their bare legs around a man's waist to gain a moment's relief from the ropes. Tegan would do the same, which would be especially hard for the others in the pen to watch. For the victim, however, being temporarily impaled on a man's hard penis even a Roman one would be a blessed relief from the suspension pain.

Xara thought about her own recent torture on the *arcis-atrox*. She knew that the centurion had never intended to kill her only to make her surrender to him. He had wanted her to submit, not to die. Tegan's torture was very different. The monster Metella intended her to die with the greatest possible pain. There was no possibility of a repreive. Her suffering and death would underscore the warning he had given today and whatever message he inteded to convey tomorrow morning.

She turned away from the cross and her eyes found Princess Ailios who was also watching the girl closely. She seemed unaffected by the horror. Tegan's day of pain was of no consequence to her, just as her father's order to sacrifice the tribe's women and children had meant nothing to her. The Romans were cold-blooded and vicious, but the Britons, her own people, had many of the same savage instincts. Were we really all that different, she wondered?

Tegan screamed desperately as her legs slipped down the side of the upright beam and her suffering arms again took her weight. Viper, standing at her front, took a step back to admire his work. The girl was a real beauty, young and strong, she would probably last until sunset, he guessed, although one could never be sure. The trick was in the ropes. Many men spread their victim's arms too far apart, thinking that it would be harder for them to pull themselves up. This was wrong, the right angle for the arms, whether it was done with ropes or nails, was forty-five degrees. This angle allowed the victim to use his or her chest, shoulder, arm, and many other muscles effectively to relieve the strain on her lungs. This better distribution of the load greatly increased the time of suffering. Even if the Catuvellauni bitch didn't last until morning as the centurion wanted, her last few hours would be an agony beyond description.

But he still needed to be careful if he was going to extract the maximum pain from her. For example, he would need to watch the men carefully. While they were fucking her, the pain in her arms would ease, but some men sometimes found it exciting to pull down on her torso just before climax to obtain a final painful squeeze of their cocks. This he could not allow. The centurion wanted her to suffer until sunrise, to achieve this, she needed to expire slowly. Pulling on her body would shorted that time.

He moved back girl's front, his eyes level with hers, and stared at her. She was shaking with fear and pain but still strong...just the way he liked them. He pushed aside his girdle and shoved his erect cock into her, lifting her

140

body a few inches higher. She tried to twist aside, but it was useless. Once he was inside her vagina, she was helpless. His hands went to her generous tits and her nipples.

Suddenly, she was moving wildly, rubbing her body against his. Viper had seen this before, the instinct to get one last taste of pleasure. He smiled as she shuddered, as trembling arousal racked her body. This was the way it was in the beginning, he knew. Pain often intesified sex especially when the torture was sensual and slow. Tegan, a virgin, screamed as his cock broke her hymen and shamefully she wrapped her log legs around his waist and began to fuck him with an impossible urgency.

Witnessing this, Princess Ailios shook her head and walked away, dismissing the girl as a shameful whore. Xara could feel the anger rising in her chest. There were no rules of conduct for someone dying on the cross. She turned back to see Viper and Tegan coming...together. Bright red blood stained the wood between the girl's clutching legs. Viper lingered a while longer, leaning on her long body, enjoying the trembling of her muscles.

"I'm afraid you must suffer a long time, my beauty," he whispered into her ear. "But keep your hope. I promise you that your suffering will end when the sun rises. There will be no lingering pain for you. I will see to it personally."

She caught her breath for a moment, "M...mer...mercy, soldier...."

Viper retrieved his cock, stood back, and smiled as he straightened his girdle. He didn't need to understand her language to know what she had asked him.

"You would not believe how many times and in how many languages I have heard those same words, beauty," he said smiling. "Keep your head, girt. My word is my bond. Your suffering will end with the new sun."

He turned towards the men waiting in clusters nearby.

"The lot of you can now take your turns, but only one man each hour. The centurion wants her to live until morning, which means we are going to have to spread out our 'relief' over that time. You, organize the sequence. Also, if I see any man pulling on her to increase his climax, I will have him flogged."

The senior man in the squad turned towards the others. Xara knew they would organize themselves in good Roman order for the fucling and take their turns by rank then by seniority. Everything in the legion was done by rank and seniority, even fucking.

Xara knew it would be a long day, the longest of Tegan's short life.

Metella returned to the horse pen at sunrise as promised. The girl was still alive but breathing in short painful gasps. The legionaries had kept her alive for twenty-four hours by fucking her every hour. They were tired of the game now; there was no pleasure in fucking someone so close to death and so nearly lifeless.

Everyone inside the compound was awake and staring sullenly out through the fence. They were standing in vigil waiting for Tegan to take her last breath. Xara stood closest staring at the Romans with undisguised hatred and contempt. Princess Ailios stood back a short distance surrounded by her entourage.

Viper unsheathed his *gladius* and stared at the rising sun. It wasn't clear to him when he should end her pain, so he waited. The moment the sun was fully above the horizon and over the eastern stockade wall, Metella

142

nodded. Viper walked to her and placed his hand on her bare chest. He could feel the slow labored breathing, the uneven fluttering of her heart.

"She lives," he announced to Metella, "but just barely. We did it, Centurion."

The men smiled and slapped each other on the back; Viper smiled as well; Metella just nodded without expression. The sergeant had timed her terrible torture nearly to the second. Slowly, he pushed the short sword into her chest just below the ribs. Her body jerked, sucked in a final breath, and slumped down for the last time. Viper pulled out his sword then cut the major artery in her leg and a significant volume of blood drained out onto the ground, marking the spot for the next victim.

Viper gestured for two of his men to remove the body. They would leave the cross upright and use stools and a ladder to crucify the next. He wasn't sure what the centurion's game was with these animals, but he was content with this light duty. Female crucifixions were easy, unlike the death struggles of a strong man. With men, he would be lucky to crucify a hundred prisoners a day; with women, all they needed was a steady supply of new bodies.

Chapter Nine - The Throne

Metella stood on the platform but didn't say anything. He wanted everyone to feel the full impact of the girl's suffering, shame, and death. Xara's rage at both the centurion and Ailios, however, was boiling over.

"You killed her, Princess," Xara shouted, loudly enough for everyone to hear. "Her name was Tegan. She suffered and died for your fucking pride."

Everyone was listening now, terrified that they would be next.

"We lost the battle," Xara continued in a rage. "The Romans defeated us. The Catuvellauni Tribe and its precious honor are no more. There is no shame in admitting this now, in bowing before the Roman in surrender. He will put all of us on the cross and make us suffer as she did unless you accede to his demands. Why must we all die...this way?"

The women in the pen were turning towards one another. Xara's diatribe had stunned them; no one had ever spoken to Ailios this way. Xara's boldness in confronting the princess, even more than her words, underscored the danger they faced. Slowly, everyone began to realize that they were each destined to experience Tegan's terrible death.

"Please, Princess," Xara pleaded, changing her tone. "I beg you, let us live. There is nothing to be gained by more death—not freedom, not honor, not satisfaction, nothing, only unnecessary pain."

Xara had a momentary flashback to the night she had kicked the centurion for no reason other than rage...and pride. Was she really any better than Ailios? Yes, I am, she decided. I acted for myself. No one else suffered because of what I did. Ailios is putting all of us on the cross.

The princess stared blankly at her for a moment then turned her back and walked away. Xara, looked helplessly at the other women then turned away as well and walked away to her own corner, defeated. She no longer feared Ailios henchmen smothering her in her sleep; murder simply wasn't on the agenda now that the other women understood the price Ailios expected them to pay for her pride.

Centurion Marcus Metella crucified two more women that day and four more the day after. Each morning, Xara made an increasingly more impassioned plea to Ailios to surrender, without success. The princess was adamant that there would be no loss of honor in front of the Romans…even if they all had to die.

By the evening of the third day, there were four crosses in the yard. Xara had become more than a translator; she was now the unofficial spokesperson for the survivors in addressing Ailios. Personally, she wanted to survive to escape and kill more Romans, but the other girls n the pen just wanted to live. As her level of desperation to convince the princess rose, she unconsciously adopted several of the same arguments the centurion had used the first morning he spoke. It wasn't until later that she realized that they were, in a strange way, working towards the same goal.

***

Princess Ailios awoke before sunrise on the fourth day just as a girl was stuffing a cloth into her mouth. Two others were holding her arms and a third moved quickly to sit on her legs. One of the princess's attendants was lying on the ground, her neck twisted to the side and drooping back at an impossible angle; other girls in Xara's party were forcefully gagging and restraining the other two loyal attendants.

Xara, clearly the attacker who had killed the first attendant, knelt beside Ailios head.

"We choose not to die for your honor, Princess," Xara whispered. "We also think that you before dying, you should suffer as the seven women your pride has killed suffered."

There was rage in Ailios eyes but now also fear. Xara was sorry that the actions of Caratacus's daughter had forced her to take this action, but she was even sorrier that it had taken her so long to act. She would always have the seven hideous deaths on her conscience; she could not wait any longer. The Roman devil was serious, he would crucify all of them.

Xara cocked her head to the side and her supporters dragged the three bound women into the central space near Metella's platform. The sun wasn't up yet, and it was a dark moonless night; the Roman guards outside the gate couldn't see what they were doing.

"Put them on their knees and tie their ankles to their thighs," Xara whispered and the others rushed to obey. Xara's leadership gave them hope that they would avoid tomorrow's crucifixions. They were ready to do whatever she asked to achieve that result.

Xara held up a sharpened stake about a foot long in front of Ailios's face.

"Here is your throne, Princess. I hope you sit on it for a long time."

146

She nodded and three of the assailants forced Ailios to lean forward. Xara took a deep breath, felt for the girl's asshole, and pushed the end of the sharpened stake into the hole with a steady pressure. Ailios jerked wildly and tried to scream through the gag. Her eyes bugged out as she faded into unconsciousness from the pain. Xara used the time to set the stake firmly into a small hole already dug in the ground. They did the same to the two girls who had remained fiercely loyal to the princess.

When Ailios regained consciousness, she felt a fire burning between her legs. Instinctively, she tried to rise on her haunches and move away from the pain, but she could only rise a few inches. The ropes holding her thighs to her ankles prevented her from lifting herself higher, from relieving the pain of the stake in her ass.

Xara was kneeling at her side.

"You are already dead, Princess. Your royal shit has now mixed with and poisoned your royal blood. The only question is how much pain you will endure before you die. Your feet and your legs will support most of your weight for another hour or two, but when they tire, you will sit back on the stake and the weight of your body will push it farther inside. The natural toughness of your intestines and other internal organs will resist its point...for a while, but eventually, it will penetrate everything. At some point the stake will penetrate something vital and you will die."

Ailios was listening with the desperation of someone suffering excruciating pain. She began to nod her head vigorously, trying to say she would concede if Xara stopped the pain.

147

"It's too late for that," Xara said. "What would we tell the spirits of the seven girls who have already died for you?"

Xara turned away then suddenly turned back.

"A courageous person would sit back hard right now, accept the greater pain and be dead in an hour. A coward like you is too afraid to do that; you will try to resist the pain for as long as possible and ultimately suffer more. Your pain, a coward's pain, might last for days.

Ailios was moaning now and shaking her head as tears streamed out of her eyes.

"It's a terrible dilemma, I admit. But ending it quickly is an option that was denied the seven who you allowed to die on the cross."

Ailios's attendants, impaled like her, were listening closely to Xara's explanation, straining to remain high on their haunches. One of them leaned back and shook violently as the stake penetrated her liver. As Xara had predicted, she was dead within the hour.

"There's one other possibility," Xara said. "If your legs can survive the burning until morning, there's a hope that the Romans will free you."

She sat back and crossed her legs to watch.

"I am thinking about all the innocents who died for your pride, Princess. They are here now with me visiting their justice on you. I sincerely hope you suffer as much as they did. I am also thinking about Caratacus, your father. It was in memory of him, of our deep affection for each other that kept me from doing this earlier. I am ashamed now for waiting so long. He would not have wanted me to wait."

She stepped away then sat cross-legged on the ground facing Ailios, watching her suffer.

The sun rose slowly in the eastern sky as they waited. When there was enough light for the Roman guards to see what was happening in the pen, there was a flurry of activity, but no one entered the pen to stop it. Viper's order was that they wait for the centurion.

Metella arrived on schedule when the sun was fully over the horizon. He paused then walked slowly to where Princess Ailios was kneeling. She was trembling with the effort to keep her weight off the stake. The agony on her face was terrible. He removed her gag.

"Please, I surrender, Roman. Help me," she said desperately in the Catuvellauni language, which Xara translated with exaggerated correctness, emphasizing each word as if she were the one suffering. The stake had penetrated deeply into Ailios's body during the night. But it was the slow tearing of her asshole that was causing the continuous pain, her organs had very few nerves. A quick flicker of a Roman sword now would be a tender mercy, Xara thought. Marcus turned and stared at Xara sitting cross-legged in front of the girl. She looked back at him with a neutral expression.

"Do you beg for Roman mercy, Princess?" Marcus asked loudly, and Xara dutifully translated.

Princess Ailios looked up at him hopefully and nodded yes. The rest of the woman were listening to the exchange, too afraid to interfere.

Metella turned to Viper.

"Make a note, Sergeant, and get some men to witness it that Princess Ailios of the Catuvellauni Tribe begged for Roman mercy on her knees on the fourth day of her captivity." He turned to the assembled women. "As is our custom, since your sovereign's legal surrogate has begged for mercy, it shall be granted to all of you...today at sunset."

The assembled throng let out a collective sigh of relief not immediately realizing the implication for the two women on the stakes."

"Sun...sunset," Ailios croaked. "I cannot wait until sun..."

"Leave these three where they are until sunset," Metella ordered loudly. "They made us wait three days, they can wait one."

Princess Ailios raised her head in despair and wailed piteously. The awful sound carried outside the horse pen and several soldiers passing by looked up then went back to their work. For Ailios, sunset was a pain-filled lifetime away. Marcus cast one more glance at Xara then walked out of the horse pen. Xara stared at his back, suddenly glad that he had not granted mercy to the merciless Ailios.

What had all of this been about? She wondered. She knew that the Romans never allowed legal niceties to take priority over practical realities. The centurion had killed seven Catuvellauni women and forced Xara to kill four others, all of whom the Romans could have easily sold as slaves. Why? What was his purpose?

***

True to his word, Metella returned to the pen at sunset and had the three whom Xara had impaled untied, including Princess Ailios. One had died by her own hand by sitting back on her stake, but Ailios and one other were still alive. By that time, however, their stakes were far inside their bodies.

In an act of mercy or perhaps just impatience, Metella ordered their stakes removed. The two girls writhed in the dust screaming in pain. They died minutes later from loss of blood. Xara was satisfied, they had delivered justice to the guilty. Ailios and her retainers had paid in full for the lives they had wasted.

"There will not be any more crucifixions," Metella declared. "However, the slave known as Xara is responsible for killing the princess, and for destroying three other slaves who belonged to the legion. She must pay for these crimes. I will take one other from the group in retaliation."

He pointed at one of the girls, the one named Vela, and turned to Viper.

"Take them."

Viper followed Metella to a stand of trees just outside the stockade, where Metella ordered him to chain Xara naked to a tree trunk. The torches the men carried cast a fiery yellow light over everything.

The devil will torture and kill me now," Xara thought, "perhaps the same way I killed Ailios. It will be an ignoble, horrifying death, but one I probably deserve. He had condemned me to suffer and die that first night for kicking him. Now...now that I've served his purpose, whatever it was, he is going to carry out his original sentence. Surprisingly, the one thing she regretted was the public aspect of her execution.

If he took me to his tent, she thought, I would at least be able to fuck him again. I would have liked another night with the centurion, perhaps one that ended with a powerful thrust from his sword. That would be a death I could embrace.

151

She understood why it could not happen this way. She was guilty of too many Roman crimes. She was an enemy, and the Romans savored watching the final agony of a hated enemy. Viper, who had been talking on the side to Metella while other men chained her to the tree, pushed the bound Vela forward.

"Do it," Metella ordered.

Viper roughly positioned Vela facing Xara then forced her to extend her arms to the side in a "T" position. He quickly attached leather shackles hanging by ropes from two low lying branches to her wrists. When the terrified girl was secure, he looked back at the Centurion who nodded. One arm at a time, they slowly elevated her so that her toes were just a few inches off the ground. The pull of the straps forced her naked body hard against Xara's. Her mouth was within inches of the girl's ear.

Xara could hear her panting, feel her sharp round breasts punctuated by her hard pebble-like nipples pressing into her; she could imagine the tiny prick of the girl's clit standing erect. It was a strange bondage. What did the monster Metella have planned for them?

"I need a translator," the centurion said slowly and clearly over Vela's shoulder in Latin. "The Legion has business with the tribes in the North and I need someone who can accurately change my words to theirs while we negotiate.

"If you agree to perform this service for me, this girl will live. If not, she will die slowly of strangulation as her arm and chest muscles weaken. Her death will be a crucifixion except you will experience her torture; you will feel everything she feels. We can keep her alive for days, and you will feel every moment of her pain."

152

Vela was staring directly into Xara's eyes, pleading with her.

"Your answer...?"

Xara stared at him. She wanted to scream her defiance, to explain how Romans were the scum of the earth, inhuman beasts, torturers who had neither heart nor conscience...but Vela's trembling body and pleading eyes were already exerting their influence. Too many Catuvellauni girls had already died; too many innocents had already suffered too much. The Roman was never going to give up.

"*Ignavus* (coward)."

The word passed over her lips and seemed to hang in the dense night air,

Viper stepped closer, prepared to punish Xara for her insolence, but Marcus held up his hand.

"Leave us," he ordered.

Viper stared at him for a moment then gathered his men and left. Xara could feel Vela's pain as the straps pulling at her arms continued to crush her lungs.

"You are a warrior, Xara," Metella whispered over Vela's bare shoulder, "more of a warrior than many of the Catuvellauni men, but you are also a woman...as we both know. Will you really allow this innocent girl to die for the sake of your pride? Are you that much like Princes Ailios?"

The question hung in the air between them, highlighted by Vela's moans.

"Do you feel her muscles beginning to tremble...her nipples hardening...her clit extending? In a short time, she will try to relieve the pain of her suspension by wrapping her legs around your body. This will be even more disturbing for you. The worst part will come when she is

153

no longer able to hang onto you; that will be the moment when she understands that her fate is to suffocate slowly. She will stare into your eyes then and ask, why? Why did I have to die this way?"

He stopped and let her absorb his words.

"You should prepare an answer for her and for the others. I am prepared to crucify all of the women in the horse pen to secure your agreement." He walked away and began to make a fire. "I will stay her until the girl is dead then we will return to the stable and crucify the others. You will watch each of them die. You can stop it whenever you want, or…"

He stopped talking. There was nothing left to say. Xara's eyes followed him with undisguised hatred.

Marcus poked at the fire and Vela's body twitched at the sound. Xara could feel every part of her even her full lips which were brushing against her earlobe.

"Why…why am I dying like this, Xara?" she asked in a whisper. "Why…? Was it for helping you kill Princess Ailios? Why has the Roman hung me this way…pressed up against you like this?"

Shhh, Xara answered.

She could literally feel the girl's pain. Her muscles were straining now, pulling hard against the constant tug of the leather. They won't last much longer, Xara thought. She could already feel the girl's bare legs opening, preparing to take over when her arms and shoulders gave out. There was wetness near Vela's cunt. She had already come quietly while the centurion was talking.

"Help me, please. I don't want to die…this way. Please."

Vela's simple plea, the stress in her voice cut Xara like a knife. She would not be able to speak in a while.

154

She could feel her legs opening, trying to grip the tree trunk at her back. She was pressing her churning cunt into Xara's stomach. Was she going to let her die...so that she did not betray herself to the Roman? Wasn't he right? Didn't that make her like Ailios?

Xara didn't answer Vela's question. She could feel the girl's wet tears on her face. She could feel her lung laboring, her drool falling on her shoulder, her heart beating faster; she could feel the girl's wet cunt sucking on her abs in a kind of nervous pre-fucking motion.

"He wants me to help him," Xara answered, unable to keep silent, "and I cannot. I hate Romans. I have sworn never to surrender to them, never to..."

Vela's body stiffened then the muscle in her right arm began to spasm. She moaned weakly, desperately trying to relieve the pressure on the twisting muscle but unable to do that without pulling harder on the other strap. It was an excruciatingly painful dilemma. As a last resort she tried to wrap her legs more tightly around Xara's waist...just as the centurion had predicted.

"Please, Xara, help me...!" she said in a way that was half a scream and half a plea for mercy. "PLEASE!"

Xara wrestled with her conscience then she called out to Metella. He stood up and walked to her.

"I am listening," he said quietly, chewing on a piece of dried meat.

Xara closed her eyes then spoke in a hollow voice devoid of all feeling.

"Let her live, Roman, let all of them live, and I will do as you ask. I continue to hate Romans and I will kill you at the first opportunity, but I will do what you want."

Could it be, she wondered, amazed. Did he do all this, did he kill all these women just to get her to

155

translate. She suddenly understood. She would never have agreed to work for the Romans otherwise. She would have died first. For the first time, she understood that the Roman was not just a devil, he was also clever. Far too clever to trust.

"I will take you at your word, Xara, and you shall have your reward," Metella said, reaching up to untie Vela's ropes. The girl crumpled to her knees at Xara's feet. She was struggling to breathe and crying hysterically in relief. Metella grabbed her hair and pushed her face into Xara's cunt.

"Meet your god, bitch. She has saved you. I suggest you use your remaining strength to please her."

He pushed Vela's face hard into Xara's cunt and held it there. Vela, thinking that the cunnilingus was part of the requirement to escape execution, began to fiercely lick Xara's labia and suck on her clit. The intensity of it was overwhelming.

"You owe me nothing, Vela," Xara shouted at her. "Stop…STOP! This is between me and the Roman. It has nothing to do with you. He wants me to…"

But Vela was too aroused. In her mind, Xara's climax equaled her salvation, her escape from an excruciating death. Her tongue flicked mindlessly in and out of Xara's cunt. Her lips kept sucking on…

"Please…stop…"

Instead of stopping, Vela increased the intensity, alternating frantically between sucking lovingly on her clit and running her tongue deep inside her cunt. Xara began to move her midsection in time to Vela's rhythm. Metella watched, his arms crossed. It wasn't the same feeling as a cock, but the image of the beautiful girl on her knees with her arms forcefully outstretched,

156

worshiping her with her tongue and her lips was intoxicating…arousing.

When Vela bent her head back to reach Xara's asshole with her mouth, Xara came in a glorious shuddering that shook her body from head to toe. It wasn't the same kind of climax she'd experienced with the centurion. That had felt like a large beast was shaking her to pieces. This was gentler, more tremulous, like someone was wrapping her in a warm blanket after a cold swim.

Vela put her wet face against the side of Xara's thigh and rested, still suspended on her knees by the leather. Xara, still feeling the contractions of her orgasm, stared down at the girl's young body, at her breasts, her face, her long hair.

"Your orgasm seals our bargain, Xara." Metella said quietly untying Vela's ropes.

There was no need for more words between them. Xara had saved Vela from a terrible death, and the girl had responded with the naturally submissive act the Romans called cunnilingus. Xara had surrendered twice tonight, once in agreeing to the centurion's terms and once to Vela's probing tongue.

He was right, again, her orgasm was a fitting way to seal her bargain with the Devil.

THE END OF BOOK 1

Read more of She-Wolf in Book 2 of the series...
The Centurion